MY UNCLE JOHN IS A ZOMBIE!

JOHN A. RUSSO

Burning Bulb
PUBLISHING

My Uncle John Is A Zombie!
By **John A. Russo**

Burning Bulb Publishing
P.O. Box 4721
Bridgeport, WV 26330-4721
United States of America
www.BurningBulbPublishing.com

PUBLISHER'S NOTE: This book is a work of fiction. Names, characters, places, and incidents are either the product of the author's imagination or are used fictitiously, and any resemblance to actual persons, living or dead, events, or locales is purely coincidental.

Cover designed by Gary Lee Vincent.

First Edition.

Paperback Edition ISBN: 978-1-948278-04-1

Printed in the United States of America

PROLOGUE

By John A. Russo

This book is a collaboration between me and Uncle John, and I feel honored that he asked me to participate. The public period of his undead life lasted only seven months, and before that he was in hiding for twelve years. Now he is in hiding once again because he narrowly escaped people out to do him harm.

He approached me quite cautiously about doing this book with him, because he respected my credentials but feared what my attitude toward him might be. I assured him that I wanted to help him tell his remarkable story, and I also wanted to atone for the unfair way that I portrayed folks like him back in the days when I was so unsympathetic to their plight. I'm ashamed that I openly revealed my prejudice against them in my book, *Night of the Living Dead.*

Fifty years ago, as the whole world knows, there was a devastating zombie apocalypse. It was brought under control for a while, but the dead didn't stay dead. The Zombie Disease kept on erupting anywhere and everywhere and nobody knew how or why. There was no treatment and no cure. Every time there was an epidemic, the flesh-eating ghouls were destroyed with guns, clubs and torches. But even when the authorities reported that all the ghouls had been killed, people were afraid that some of them had merely gone into hiding, helped by their loved ones, who wanted to protect them instead of driving spikes into their heads or tossing them onto a bonfire. Over the years, there were persistent rumors about zombies who had recovered their human faculties and could actually walk and talk, and maybe even have sex, while they persisted in satisfying their cannibalistic cravings.

Uncle John was the first of these creatures to actually come forward. And he caused a sensation. Due to his mushrooming notoriety, he acquired numerous detractors and admirers, but also fanatical enemies. In the face of it all, he remained cheerful and optimistic.

1

This is his true story told mostly in his own words, which I dutifully transcribed and then embellished, admittedly, for the sake of marketability. Ninety percent of the source material came either from his own mouth or from insights furnished by his niece and nephew, who have always been his caregivers and protectors. For the other roughly ten percent, dealing with events that they did not personally witness, I relied on videotapes that survived a rampage at a zombie hunting camp, and on interviews with jailhouse snitches. My efforts were aided and abetted by a highly dedicated police officer, Detective Jane Smart, who started out as Uncle John's nemesis but eventually became his friend and ally -- and much more, as you will see.

Please bear in mind that what happened to Uncle John was not his fault. He's suffering from a terrible disease that everybody fears and nobody understands except in a vague way. But the uplifting thing is that, through it all, he has not lost his humanity. He's still a caring person with penetrating insights and a sharp sense of humor spiced with his own brand of sarcasm.

CHAPTER 1

In the Cemetery

My niece and nephew kept me safe for a good part of my undead life. Cy-Fi is ditzy but she has a good heart. Oscar isn't the brightest bulb in the chandelier, but he's a security guard and he has a permit to carry a gun, and he'd give his life to protect me. I raised them both after their parents were killed in an auto accident when they were toddlers. As grown-ups, they hid me after I became infected and helped me satisfy my special appetite.

I don't know how I got this way. I woke up one morning and my hands and feet were numb. I wiggled my toes, thought it'd go away, but then a terrible craving came over me. I wanted to bite into somebody soft and tender looking, but I was so slow and awkward that I couldn't catch anybody. Some little kid's father was going to conk me over the head with an iron pipe, but Cy-Fi and Oscar saved me just in the nick of time. They judo-chopped that guy. Then they nursed me and took care of me the best they could.

Last year was the 50th anniversary of *Night of the Living Dead*, the movie that chronicled the very first zombie outbreak, and so Cy-Fi got it into her ditzy little brain to invite a TV crew to the Evans City Cemetery, where that creepy movie was filmed, to introduce the entire world to me in hopes that they'd see how intelligent I am and realize that zombies should be treated more humanely. She said that everybody was so used to zombies by now that they'd be more open to her point of view, but I thought she was overreaching, to put it mildly. She promised that she and Oscar would stay close to me at all times, and Oscar would have his gun handy -- but what if somebody was lurking in the woods and zeroing in on me with deer rifle with a telescopic sight?

Just so you won't hate me, let me make one thing perfectly clear. I don't like to eat the kind of food that I have to eat, but it tastes good and it stops me from rotting. Cy-Fi believes that her herbal concoctions and magical spells are what caused me to regain some of my human attributes, especially my speech faculty. But I tend to think that it occurred naturally with the passage of time, just as the brain will partially heal itself after a stroke. Like other dead people, I stopped aging. But my fingers are always stiff, and my face is purplish and a touch rotted.

I can't type on a computer keyboard, because of my fingers. I believe there's a device you can talk into that changes speech into words, and I think that's what Stephen Hawking uses. But I'm technology impaired and I didn't want to have to get used to that kind of contraption. So I'm dictating this stuff to John Russo. I hope he listens carefully and gets it right.

I was scared and worried on our long drive to the cemetery, and I was in no hurry to get out of the car when Oscar and Cy-Fi did. A lot roomier than most sedans nowadays, it was a 1967 LeMans, pale green with a dark green top, like the one used in the opening scene in *Night of the Living Dead*. I have no idea why she wanted that car, in light of the atrocities that movie perpetrated. The ghouls in it were treated like dumb brutes with something far worse than Mad

Cow disease. They were shot in the head, piled up like cordwood, doused with kerosene and set ablaze. Troubled by awful thoughts of that sort, I was cowering in the backset of Cy-Fi's Pontiac when she said, "Good, they're not here yet, Oscar. We have time to get ready."

"Get ready how?" he asked, in his perplexed way.

"Well, we don't want the TV crew to see Uncle John right off the bat. We have to make sure they aren't being followed."

"By who?"

"By the cops, dummy!"

"Okay, Sis."

Cy-Fi and I were both worried that somebody at the TV station might've told the cops that I was claiming to be a real zombie. If they got a close look at me, they might just gun me down without taking any chances.

"Get moving, Oscar," Cy-Fi said. "Go hide and keep your eyes peeled for a cop car."

I didn't see how Oscar was going to protect me. His security guard uniform wouldn't cut any ice. A wannabe cop, he had failed the exam three times, and anyhow he was too pudgy. He often jogged with me in an attempt to lose a few pounds, but then he'd eat a gallon of chocolate ripple ice cream. Cy-Fi wanted to look beautiful for the television camera, so she was wearing a black and gray pleated gown over a laced-up corset that she didn't need because she had an hourglass figure without it. She wore black lipstick, black nail polish, black eye shadow and green-and-black eye liner. Her hair was long, black and luxuriant.

She had to help me get out of the car because my limbs were more rigor-mortised than usual from the long, uncomfortable ride. Seeing the look of trepidation on my face, she said, "Come on out, Uncle John. Don't worry, I'll make sure nobody hurts you." I had my doubts, and my breathing was slow and raspy because I was so scared and tired. She led me toward a large graveyard monument, then said, "Duck behind here till I tell you to come out, Uncle John. Don't make any noise or they might hear you. Try not to breathe so loud." Easier said than done. But I hunkered down behind the monument just in time as a TV van pulled into the cemetery. Cy-Fi eyed it warily, and Oscar watched from where she had posted him, his hand on his holstered pistol.

Mandy Frost, a gorgeous redhead I recognized from her nightly program on FLSH-TV, got out of the van with a guy toting a big video camera. I peeped from behind the monument and saw them approach.

"I'm Mandy Frost," Mandy said, "and this is my cameraman, Steve Munch. You promised us an interview with your Uncle John, but I don't see him anywhere."

5

"First I have to make sure we can trust you," said Cy-Fi. "You can do my interview first, then him. Ask me anything you want, as long as you don't set the cops onto us."

"Hmph!" Mandy said snootily. "They'll see you on television, and I can't help that. Your interviews are worth nothing to us if we can't put them on the air. How you manage to hide from the cops is your own damned business. You either want the publicity or you don't."

Steve Munch said, "Mandy, let's get you and Cy-Fi into a nice two-shot in front of that tall tombstone. I'm ready to roll when you are."

Mandy drew herself up and smiled winningly. "This is Mandy Frost on location for an exclusive interview with a young woman who calls herself Cy-Fi. She won't tell me her real name or where she lives. But she claims to have an uncle -- her Uncle John that is -- who got zombified during an outbreak a dozen years ago. Cy-Fi, you claim that your uncle has survived without being shot in the head or burned in a bonfire?"

"Yes, Mandy, and I want you to know that he could not have survived without my help. The whole world is callous toward zombies, as if they're not really *human!* I love Uncle John dearly. When I was a little girl, he bought me popsicles and gave me piggyback rides. And he adopted me and my brother when our parents were killed in an accident. It's not his fault what he turned into. He deserves to be hospitalized and treated, not hunted down and shot."

Mandy Frost said, "Your uncle is dangerous, isn't he? Won't he bite people and give them the zombie disease?"

"He will do that, I have to admit," said my niece. "But I make sure he only bites people who deserve it."

"Well, my gosh! Most of our viewers would be appalled to hear you say that! What kind of people would you say *deserve* to be *ghoul*-bitten?"

"Child rapists...serial killers...Republicans..."

"*Republicans?* Why on earth...?"

"They don't want zombies to have health care. They don't want *anybody* to have health care. Anybody but *them*. Most zombies come from the middle class or lower, not the upper-class, much less the top one percent."

"Well, how do we know all this isn't just a big put-on? How do we know your Uncle John is really a zombie? Can we talk to him? You call yourself Cy-Fi -- science *fiction!* Fess up -- it's all just a big put-on, *isn't* it?"

By now Oscar had come close enough to hear her, and he got miffed. "We could prove Uncle John is a real zombie," he said, "by letting him bite you or your cameraman -- *then* wait and see what happens."

Mandy's eyes widened at the mere thought of it, and Cy-Fi said, "Calm down, Oscar, and be nice." Then she looked toward where I was hiding and said, "Come on out, Uncle John. I won't let them hurt you."

She took my hand and led me into the camera setup, and I felt as shaky as a beaten dog. Mandy and Munch were obviously taken aback, looking at my half-rotted face and fearing not only that I might be real but that I might be dangerous.

Mandy pulled herself together and said, "You said I could talk to him. But can he talk back?"

"Yes, he can," Cy-Fi said proudly, "and I don't know why exactly. Most zombies aren't really able to say much except for the ones who scream for human brains. But Uncle John has

his speech faculty, maybe because I give him the right things to eat, and maybe because he was so intelligent before he got sick."

"That seems farfetched," Mandy said perfunctorily. "How do I know your uncle isn't just an actor in makeup?"

"How'd you like me to bite your neck?" I blurted at her.

"Don't be scared, Mandy, he's only kidding!" Cy-Fi interjected. " But after all, he does need to eat, just like any of God's creatures. People talk about endangered species like lions and tigers. But what about zombies? Nobody's more endangered than *they* are! Zombies are human *beings*. They need help."

Mandy said, "I hear what you're saying, but it's too much for me to digest. I can run this as a human interest story, but I don't think anyone's going to buy into it as a piece of genuine investigative journalism." Then, probing further, she said, "Uncle John, do you remember how you acquired the zombie disease in the first place?"

I told her about waking up with my hands and toes going numb. Then she asked me the same question she had asked Cy-Fi about the kind of people I go after in order to satisfy my special hunger, and I reiterated that I only devour people who deserve it, like rapists, murderers and child molesters. I was mostly telling the truth. And I didn't think I deserved to be shot for it; in fact I felt that I was performing a public service. Even as a zombie I clung to core principles that were ethical and honorable, even though I had been forced to modify them somewhat due to my circumstances. I used to be against the death penalty, but I had come to believe that it was appropriate for folks who were so inhumane that they couldn't be rehabilitated. And I didn't think that zombies like myself deserved capital punishment, because our cravings for human flesh were not our fault; the affliction was not one that we would have willfully chosen.

Like me, Cy-Fi had a good heart. She liked the fact that zombies existed because to her they were proof of the supernatural and thus seemed to give credence to her belief in magical spells and potions. On a more pragmatic level, she wanted laws passed to protect the Undead, federal money appropriated for research into potential cures, hospitals established for the afflicted, and hospices available for those who were doomed.

She led an unorthodox life, as did I. But she was a crusader, trying to do her best for me and people like me, and I loved her for it.

CHAPTER 2

A Hardnosed Detective Zeroes in on Me

As luck would have it, I was seen on TV by a blonde, beautiful homicide detective named Jane Smart, who had a grudge against zombies. And later that night, she was called to the scene of a body dump. It was at the edge of the woods surrounding a small playground. Two uniforms were already there, along with a patrol car, a morgue wagon, a coroner and two assistants. The body was that of a twenty-something man wearing a tight black T-shirt, ragged jeans and sockless sneakers. There was a bloody bullet hole in the corpse's back, and the pudgy baldheaded coroner, Ted Blankley, was looking down at it as Detective Smart ducked under the crime-scene tape.

Squinting into the strobe-lights of the squad car and the overpowering brightness of the tungsten lamps set up on stands, Jane said, "What've we got, Ted?"

"Dead as a doornail," Blankley said. "No rigor mortis yet. Probably shot less than four hours ago. Help me turn him over, Jane."

She glanced at the two attendants, as if wondering what they were there for and why she was being asked to do their job, before helping Ted Blankley turn over the body. Then she saw that the dead man had another bullet hole in the center of his forehead. And, worse, that part of his left arm, which had been tucked under his torso, had been rudely amputated. She couldn't help blurting, "Chrissake, Ted!"

"What, Jane? You've never seen a head with a bullet in it? Or are you talking about his missing arm and hand?"

"I recognize him. It's Clyde Yancey. It pissed me off when they let him out on bail last week. He molested at least a dozen kids."

"But the way I hear, you only had circumstantial evidence. You wanted to put him away permanently, but the prosecutor wasn't sure he could convince a jury."

"Well, now he won't have to," said Jane. "Somebody did us a favor. And I have a pretty good idea who."

She was talking about me, my niece and my nephew. From that point on, she was on us like a bloodhound in heat. She was sure we must've killed Clyde Yancey so I could munch on part of him. I won't say one way or another whether we actually did it, and I'll take the Fifth if I'm ever prosecuted for it. I had no sympathy for Clyde Yancey, but I knew I had to be scared of Jane Smart when I saw her on TV talking about the Yancey case. She revealed that she had seen me on FLSH-TV, then said, "He's probably not a real zombie, just a sicko with cannibalistic delusions. But I'll kill him if I catch him taking a bite of human flesh. And I'll put him away for good if we find his DNA on Clyde Yancey's severed arm."

It made me wonder if zombies still had DNA. There were lots of things we didn't have anymore, like certain normal bodily functions, and I hoped DNA was one of them. But I made up my mind not to donate any, even if Jane Smart tried to force me to do it.

Watching Jane on TV, in spite of the danger she presented to me I must say that I found her very appealing. In hiding for twelve years, I got insanely horny, but whenever I managed to get near any pretty girls, they'd all run from me. As I already told you, one advantage of being a zombie was that I stopped aging, but still I looked horrible because of the purplish bruising and partial decay of my face. But I didn't smell bad, like a normal corpse. I suppose that was because I wasn't exactly a *normal* one.

CHAPTER 3

My Ordinary Home Life

My niece and nephew and I tried very hard to lead a normal life, especially when we were at home. We lived in a small town not far from Pittsburgh, but I'm not saying which one. We still live there now but it has to stay secret because people are still after me.

After our interview with Mandy Frost in the Evans City Cemetery ran on television it caused so much fuss that a couple of days later FLSH-TV ran a special on us, intended to milk our public debut for all it was worth. They had shot a lot of stuff on us that hadn't run the first time, so now they put the outtakes together in a longer program. Cy-Fi was anxious to see it, and so was I. But Oscar was guzzling beer and eating cheese curls and couldn't wait for it to play and be over. "When's it comin' on, Sis?" he kept nagging her. "It's time for me to watch *Hollywood Squares*."

"Shut up," she told him. "That crap went off the air ages ago."

"It's a re-run," he said, "but I still wanna watch it 'cause I know all the answers. Then I'm gonna watch one of them real-life murder stories on *ID Discovery* so I can learn more about how to out-fox the fuzz."

See what I mean? In my own home I had to constantly put up with bickering between siblings. In most ways zombies are like anyone else. We have day-to-day ordinary problems and somebody has to take out the garbage.

"After the news is over you can watch *Sesame Street*, for all I care," Cy-Fi told Oscar. "Look! There's Mandy Frost and there's us!" She was entranced, sipping wine in her pajamas, and almost spilling it on herself because she was so excited.

On the flat-screen, Mandy said to Cy-Fi, "Well, you claim you help your Uncle John get...er...food...am I right?"

"Yes, he's older now, and his teeth aren't what they used to be, and I can't take him to the dentist -- what an uproar *that* would cause. So I have to help him with his nutrition."

"She takes good care of me because she loves me," I chipped in. "I don't know what I'd do without her. She's the best niece any fellow could ever ask for."

Eyeing me warily, Mandy said, "Do you still kill and eat human beings?"

"Don't forget I'm a human being, too!" I snapped at her.

"Yes, and you have a right to live," Cy-Fi said, patting my shoulder.

"He has to kill and eat somebody *every day?*" Mandy yiped.

"Not every day, no," I told her indignantly.

"If he gets a good substantial meal," said Cy-Fi, "he can go three or four days or more on just orange juice, or better yet, a highly nutritious concoction I make in a blender -- out of milk, yogurt, bananas, and a lot of wholesome vitamins and minerals."

To tell you the truth, some of what she had told Mandy wasn't true. I mostly have to eat meat. That other kind of crap would make me sick. But I can eat other kinds of nutritious food if I do it sparingly.

Mandy was skeptical. She said, "Okay, I'll go along with the gag, but I don't really believe Uncle John is a real zombie. Let me see if I can peel off his makeup!" She reached toward my face, and I jumped back. Oscar almost drew his gun, and I cried out, "*No!* Don't touch me!"

"You promised not to invade his space!" Cy-Fi accused Mandy. "This interview is over!"

We stomped away from the camera and headed for our car, leaving Mandy there all alone, speaking into the microphone while Steve Munch filmed her solo. "This is Mandy Frost, on location. I suppose it's possible that this guy who calls himself Uncle John is an *actual* zombie who got away from the cops and the zombie-hunting vigilantes way back when. It's hard to believe, though, and I promise you I will follow up on this amazing and somewhat unnerving story."

The program cut to a commercial for panty hose, and Oscar chugged beer and stuffed cheese curls into his mouth, then reached for the remote, saying, "Now c'n I watch what *I* wanna watch?"

Cy-Fi held out the remote toward him, but then yanked it away from his grasping hand, teasing him, but finally let him have it, saying, "Here, crybaby."

"Why do you have to be so mean to me? I'm your big brother and I don't let anybody hurt you, Cy-Fi."

"I know, Oscar. I appreciate you, I really do."

"So do I," I told him, and he smiled happily.

Little did I know it at the time, but it turned out that this was just about the last peaceful day we ever had. My notoriety built and built till it became an albatross. At first some people believed I was a real zombie, and some didn't. One of the advantages of coming out was that I could let myself be seen by un-zombified humans now and then, but I had to be careful because I knew full well that somebody might try to shoot me in the head or set me on fire. The main thing that kept this from happening was the doubt in their minds as to whether or not I was the genuine article. In other words, even though they knew it was perfectly within the law to shoot a zombie, what if I was only a fake? Then it would turn out that they had committed murder and the death penalty could be imposed on *them*.

Although I was always in danger from the zombie haters out there, I relished my little tastes of freedom and worked up the nerve to start clerking part-time in Cy-Fi's store. I liked being around the lovely young women who modeled the Goth clothing and makeup that she designed. I enjoyed the wild, nutty raves that she dee-jayed, with lots of loud music and zany, bizarre people.

When I was around attractive young women, I always made sure that I wasn't really hungry at that moment. That way they weren't in any danger from me. I was appalled at the slews of politicians and show-business celebrities who were being fired for sexual misconduct. I was never the type to force my attentions on anybody. Sure, I needed love and sex, but I wanted it to be genuine, and genuinely desired by both parties. To me, a relationship with a woman was only good if it existed on a deep and mutually respectful level.

One day when I saw Jane Smart on Mandy Frost's program, talking about the notorious

Clyde Yancey case, I found her charming and likeable even though I knew she would cheerfully shoot me down if she got a chance. I always liked ballsy proactive women; they didn't scare me like they scared some men.

Questioned by Mandy as to why she was so highly dedicated, Jane readily admitted that she didn't have a boyfriend right now and didn't want one and that she scarcely had time for a personal life. I reflected that we certainly had lack of a sex life in common. And I wondered if any young, desirable woman would ever go for me. Some of the more twisted ones went for murderers, even murderers in prison, like the Melendez brothers. But Jane didn't seem twisted. She said she had gotten engaged once, but cut the relationship off when it became abusive. I figured that was a point in my favor because even though I was a zombie and not very handsome anymore, at heart I was never an abuser. Back when I was a history professor, coeds would come on to me sometimes, but I kept a safe distance. Some were just after higher grades even if they had to use sex to get them, and some maybe found me attractive, but I remained a man of principle, with, I admit, considerable difficulty at times when I had to rein in my libido.

On TV Jane Smart told Mandy Frost that during a zombie outbreak ten years earlier, she had gunned down many of the Undead. "I was driven by grief and rage because my mother was bitten by one of them and had to be shot and burned. I thought I was going to have to kill my own mom, but luckily my partner did it while I turned my head and closed my eyes."

I felt pity for her when she said all that. But when she was asked about me, her hatred was palpable. She said, "Uncle John can't possibly be a *real* zombie! His niece and nephew are charlatans, out to bilk the public -- they'll probably soon be setting up a Go Fund Me page!"

I forgave her for these false sentiments, partly because I was already smitten with her. It was perfectly understandable that she and the general public didn't know exactly what to make of me. Was I for real, or was I a fraud? And if I was an actual zombie, why could I talk? Why didn't I just shamble around and hiss and growl like all the other zombies they were used to?

In all honesty, I was just as perplexed about it as they were.

CHAPTER 4

An Abduction

While I was trying to adjust to my new life as a celebrity, I attracted the attention of a wicked 60-year-old mobster named Stush Polanski who believed that the only good zombie was a dead one. That's how people like him used to think about Native Americans. If Stush had been alive back in days of Buffalo Bill and Wild Bill Hickock, he would have been slaughtering buffalo by shooting them from railroad cars or torching and shooting Indian women and children in their tents, or perpetrating ignominious massacres like the one at Wounded Knee.

As a former history professor with a minor in political science, I tend to view current events through the prism of the past. It's my method of gaining a deeper understanding of what's going on now. When I was teaching history to college students I tried to make them realize that, as William Faulkner famously said, "The past is not only not dead, it is not even past." For instance, if the current President of the United States understood anything besides money and power and how to acquire more and more of it, we would not all be worrying about his finger being inches away from a nuclear button.

Like other villains in low places as well as high places, Stush Polanski was an embodiment of the ingrained flaws and pervasive immorality of the human race. He and his henchmen were capturing innocent victims, mostly female, and turning them into zombies or else using them for zombie feed. He was keeping dozens of hungry zombies in a cage, then turning them loose, several at a time, so that hunters with no sense of decency could gun them down and win prize money. His immorality had no bounds. He even had a couple of filmmakers shooting videos of his "zombie hunts" so he could make a fortune selling DVD's over the Internet. He called it "zombie snuff."

I have seen some of that disgusting footage. I have also read transcripts of interrogations that were conducted with Stush's accomplices either at the police station while they were being booked or later after they were sent to prison. John Russo forked out some money under the table to get hold of all this awful stuff.

This account of the kidnapping of a young woman named Betty Montgomery was given to the police by the getaway driver, Harvey Slocum, who felt so little remorse that he actually giggled while confessing to things so hideous. This is John Russo's take on Slocum's story, with embellishments that he calls "artistic license" but which I call crass exploitation:

At a cottage on a lake not far from Pittsburgh, teenager Betty Montgomery, lusciously voluptuous in a yellow bikini, stepped out into bright early-morning sunshine. With a mild after-

tingle in her private parts, she recollected the lovemaking she had indulged in the night before. It wasn't fully satisfying, but it would do. (This is what I mean by "crass exploitation." How does John Russo know exactly what the young lady's erotic thoughts may have been?)

Betty's boyfriend, a callow lad named Jimmy Butler, came out onto the porch, banging the screen door. He kissed her, forcing his tongue into her mouth, hoping she'd want to go at it again. But she pulled away, snatched a piece of paper towel from a roll on a slatted wooden tray that hung from a barbecue grille, and wiped her mouth.

Blissfully unaware of his erotic shortcomings, Jimmy said smugly, "I bet I made you forget about your crush on your faculty adviser -- right, babe?"

"Thanks to the Jack Daniel's you brought with you,"

"C'mon, Betty, you know that's not what I meant."

He grabbed her, tried to kiss her again, and once more she pushed him away. Determined to think of himself as a great lover, he said, "Maybe you're just too hung over right now, but last night you were plain wild. I bet if we take us a blanket and a bottle of JD down to the beach, sparks will fly all over again."

What sparks? she thought to herself.

To get rid of him, she said, "Why don't you go for a little swim, Jimmy, while I have some toast and coffee? I've gotta get something in my stomach."

"Then will you come down to the beach?"

"Yeah, I promise. I'll bring the booze and a blanket."

"Good deal," he said with a lecherous smirk.

He bopped down off the porch and strutted away, wearing nothing but flip-flops and cutoff jeans that showed off his nice tight butt, which he thought would help get her fired up

shrugged and went into the cottage.

He strode down to the shore and waded into the lake. At first, to get used to the very cold water, he splashed his face and chest. Then he waded out deeper, surface dived and came up

spluttering, tossing back his long wet hair which hung in a clump down to his buttocks.

He had no idea he was being watched by two of Stush Polanski's men, Joe Talerico and Dan Lancaster. Joe was tall and lanky with a tangled mess of unruly black hair, and Dan was medium height, well-built and so clean cut he could have passed as a lawyer or a Wall Street broker if he had been decked out in a suit and tie. The thugs had each done quite a few years of prison time for burglary, breaking and entering, and assault with deadly weapons. Today they were dressed for the job at hand -- murder and abduction -- and both were wearing sneakers, black hoodies and faded jeans. Their getaway driver, Harvey Slocum, a skinny punk with a rap sheet not as long as theirs, had parked Joe's van a ways back from the sandy beach. Stush had clued them in on Betty and her use of the lakeshore cottage because he knew her from the old days when he was so hard-up he was a swimming pool cleaner for her father.

Dan said, "There's the young gentleman she shacked up with, Joe. Gotta get him outta the picture."

"The boss didn't say to do that."

"Didn't say not to neither. Look at that little ass on him. Probably got a teeny-weeny dick too."

Harvey Slocum giggled but cut it short when Dan and Joe gave him a hard look.

In prison for long stretches, their sexual appetites had expanded, out of sheer need. They had gotten used to raping weaker prisoners, but they didn't think of themselves as homosexuals since when they did it to men they always fantasized that they were doing it to girls.

"Better not go extracurricular with the boy. Easier to just kill him," Dan said.Joe and Dan both got out of the van and Slocum stayed behind the wheel. The two stalkers started walking toward the lake, watching Jimmy swim and frolic around and then wade to shore.

As the boy got out of the water and slipped into his flip-flops, he spotted Joe and Dan coming toward him with sneers on their faces. Alarmed, he picked up a hefty piece of driftwood and kept it ready, at his side.

Joe said, "Don't be afraid. We just wanna ask you some questions."

Jimmy was worried but trying not to show fear. Biting back a tremor in his voice, he said, "What can I do for you?"

Dan said, "Maybe you better not ask."

He and Joe both snickered.

Joe said, "If you was ever in prison you'd know never to ask another man what you can do *for* him."

"Easiest way to get somethin' rammed where you don't want it," Dan agreed. "And I

don't mean that log in your hand, I mean a different kinda log."

The thugs laughed some more, and Jimmy got more and more worried.

Dan said, "That cottage up there is on a real lonely stretch of beach. You got a girlfriend up there?"

"No...uh...she stood me up," Jimmy lied.

"I *bet* she did," Dan said with a snicker. "I just bet she stood you *up* real good!"

Joe said, "I bet Betty's real good at makin' certain things stand up."
And Dan said, "Maybe she'll wanna stand both of *us* up too."

"Don't talk about her that way," Jimmy said without a whole lot of forcefulness.

"Aw, we're sorry," Dan said. "We didn't mean to offend your virgin ears."

Jimmy tried to skirt around the two men. But they moved to keep him hemmed in. He swung at Dan with his club, but Dan dodged and Joe judo-chopped him, and he went down, dropping his club as jagged rocks cut into his knees.

Laughing, Joe kicked Jimmy in the ribs. The boy groaned and tried to crawl. When Dan stepped up to deliver another kick, Jimmy suddenly tackled him and punched him in the face.

Joe pulled a knife out of its sheathe.

Jimmy scrambled to his feet and started to run.

Joe stood still and assumed a knife-throwing stance. Jimmy managed to get about twenty feet away. Sitting in the sand, his mouth a bit bloody, Dan chortled.

Joe threw his knife -- and it *thunked* into Jimmy's back. With a loud scream, Jimmy fell. He feebly tried to crawl away, blood streaming onto the sand.

Joe ran up and stepped on the boy's neck, holding him down like a pinned snake, pushing

his face into the sand so hard he was smothering to death, thick grains of sand being forced past his lips.

From a leather pouch on his belt, Dan pulled out a meat hook and waved it around with a flourish. "Like to use *this* on him," he said.

"I know you would," said Joe. But it'd be too messy -- leave a big incriminating blood

puddle."

"Guess I'll just stand here on his neck for a spell."

Dan did so, and Jimmy struggled for a long while, then went utterly limp. Joe and Dan grinned at each other.

Back at the cottage, Betty came out onto the porch, still in her bikini, carrying a rolled-up blanket, a beach bag and a bottle of Jack Daniel's. As she walked along the lake shore she looked left and right for Jimmy but didn't spot him. Sitting in Joe's van, Dan and Joe grinned at each other and gave a thumbs-up when she spread out her blanket and sat down, not far from where Jimmy was killed.

"Good thing we dragged his body away and scuffed sand over the blood drops," Joe whispered.

Dan grinned and nodded.

Her hand shielding her eyes, Betty peered out at the glinting water. Then she padded out to the lake, walked in up to her ankles and idly waded back and forth, gazing down the beach a few times in hopes of spotting Jimmy. But she soon ceased to care very much about him and went back to the blanket and sat. She unzipped her beach bag, took out a tube of suntan lotion and began applying it to herself.

Joe and Dan jumped down from the van, slamming the doors and startling her, making her spin around and look. As she did so, they opened the rear door of the van and lugged out a large dog cage. Dan grabbed a coil of rope from inside the van and looped it over his shoulder as he and Joe carried the cage toward Betty.

She squinted at them, alert with fear.

Joe and Dan smiled ingratiatingly at her as they set the cage down. "Your name Betty?" Dan asked.

"You got a boyfriend who came down here for a swim?" asked Joe.

"Uh-huh," Betty said warily.

Joe told her, "He went to gather some driftwood to make a lamp outta. Said to tell you if we saw you."

"Said he'd be right back," Dan added.

Betty eyed the cage suspiciously and said, "What's *that* for?"

"Our collie," Dan answered. "Broke his rope and ran off. We catch him, we're gonna have to cage him."

Carrying out the charade, Joe said, "If and *when* he comes back! It's your damn fault, Joe! I told you this rope was too damned frayed in that one spot. Mutsy is long gone."

Dan said, "Don't worry, he'll come back when he gets hungry. We'll just hafta stay here and wait."

They both sat on the dog cage and peered in opposite directions of the beach, pretending to have their eyes peeled for the fictional dog. Betty went back to massaging suntan lotion into her skin, deciding to be amused instead of frightened by these two rough-looking dudes who were actually softies in love with a collie. Dan and Joe pretended to be nonchalant about her as they ogled her with sideways glances. She smiled a bemused smile, accustomed to having her lovely young body stared at by men. She lay back and closed her eyes against the bright sun, knowing they would stare all the more openly now.

Joe yelled, "Hey, Betty, whaddaya know, here comes your boyfriend!"

She sat up -- and a noose dropped over her head. Dan hauled on the rope, tightening it around Betty's neck. Her nails broke as she clawed at it -- but Dan yanked her back and she choked and spluttered. He said, "Don't fight it, gal, we wanna take you alive." He gave the rope a couple of hard yanks, till she gave in and stopped struggling. She rolled over and lay flat on her back, still clawing at the noose and trying to suck in air.

Dan said, "Tape her mouth shut, Joe, then I'll loosen the rope."

Joe plastered a hunk of surgical tape over Betty's lips. Then they rolled her over and yanked her onto her hands and knees.

"Quick, bitch! *Crawl!*" Dan barked.

"Get in the cage!" Joe commanded.

He drew his knife and sliced the noose so roughly that the sharp blade drew blood. He and Dan kicked and prodded her till she was all the way in the cage, which was made of thick woven steel wire. They slammed and locked the door, then picked her up bodily, cage and all, and carried her toward the van. Harvey Slocum jumped out of the cab and opened the cargo door when he saw them coming. Joe and Dan put the cage inside and Slocum slammed the door.

Betty's fear reached a level of maximum hysteria when she saw Jimmy's dead body on a plastic tarp, so close to her that she could have touched it if she wasn't caged. But she didn't want to touch him. Nothing she could do for him. It was clear that he no longer had a pulse.

CHAPTER 5

Uncle John Gets High Ratings

The station manager at FLSH-TV, Don Harvey, a former anchorman, gray but still handsome at age 50, was sitting alone in a conference room. He was immaculately groomed and manicured, in a three-piece pinstriped suit with a black-and-red striped necktie. Mandy Frost and Steve Munch entered warily, not sure why their boss was calling them on the carpet. She was wearing a stunning red dress showing a lot of cleavage because she knew that kind of thing was highly titillating for male viewers. Munch was dressed in jeans and a T-shirt with the logo of GWAR, an iconoclastic heavy-metal band, and his habitual ball cap.

Don Harvey smiled at Mandy and Munch and said, "Have a seat, you two. Don't worry, you're not here to get chewed out."

They sat and Munch quipped, "You mean we're gonna get a medal?"

And Mandy said, "A certificate of appreciation?"

"You actually might, if the trend continues," said Don Harvey. "That bit you did with what's-her-name, Cy-Fi, and her so-called Uncle John has jacked up your ratings tremendously. We need more of that stuff and I want you to go out and get it, whatever it takes."

Mandy and Munch mulled this over, then Mandy said, "I'm not sure Cy-Fi will grant us another interview. She's scared that the cops will come after her, just to get to her uncle and shot him, and she might even end up as collateral damage."

Munch said, "We don't even believe she told us the truth. She told me on the phone that she's a witch and can spew fire out of her mouth."

"I've seen people do that," said Don Harvey. "It's a carnival stunt. I don't know how they do it, but it's no big deal."

"But *everything* that comes out of her mouth is kinda flaky," Munch said. "I think she's just a publicity hound. She's *using* us, boss, and she's gonna wind up making us look silly."

"Well, for the time being," said Don Harvey, "we're using her as much as she's using us. She's a big boost for our sagging ratings -- her and her zombie uncle."

Having listened to all this in contemplative silence, Mandy now said, "I don't think we should play it as if we totally believe in them when we put anything else from them on the air. She's making outlandish claims, and we're reporting them, but we're not necessarily giving them our full endorsement."

"That's exactly right," Don Harvey agreed. "What we're doing is no different than the History Channel. They blatantly run so-called documentaries about devils and angels and Bigfoot and visits to earth by aliens from outer space -- as if all that shit is true fact."

"You've got a point, boss," Munch said somberly.

"That's why I get the big bucks. Listen, I'm the program manager, so I'm the one who takes the heat if FLSH-TV doesn't suck in enough eyeballs. The sponsors crawl down my throat. You make me look good, I'll see that your show gets into Prime Time. Fair enough?"

"I hope you mean that because I'll hold you to it," Mandy said, smiling sweetly.

Don Harvey pushed his point, saying, "Uncle John is your ticket to fame, Mandy! Folks are calling in like crazy ever since we gave him a taste of exposure. Half of them are scared he's gonna spread another zombie epidemic, and the other half are laughing their asses off at him. All of them are screaming for more -- and we've gotta give it to 'em and pump our ratings as sky-high as we can."

"Well," said Mandy, "Steve and I shot a lot more stuff in the graveyard. We can keep running it in short bits to keep our audience hyped up. We can also use it to make promos."

"Now you're talking, Mandy! Let's get on the stick!" Don Harvey enthused.

CHAPTER 6

Blasting Down Zombies

It was a sunny summer Saturday, the kind of day that Betty used to spend sunbathing and swimming at her parents' cottage. But Stush's men had her tied her to a stake, still wearing her skimpy yellow bikini which was now soiled and soaked with her own urine. She kept begging for her life, to no avail. Joe and Dan just laughed at her when they tied her up. Then they moved back about fifty feet and joined other men with rifles aimed in her direction.

She shut her eyes, waiting to be shot, then she heard a chorus of hisses and growls, and her eyes snapped open.

She started screaming her head off when she saw a pack of zombies coming toward her out of the wood in their slow and shambling gait.

The only female in the group of ghouls could move faster than the males because she was younger and not so decayed. She drooled and hissed, and Betty screamed even louder.

The female zombie pounced on Betty and took a bite out of her arm, then sat back on her haunches grinning and chewing while Betty continued to groan and whimper.

Stush's voice rang out. "Okay, she's bitten! Blast away!" He didn't want the victim to be totally chewed up, just bitten enough to turn into a freshly created zombie for later use. She had been used as a lure, getting the un-caged zombies to come out of the surrounding woods, and now the hunters were free to shoot.

A fusillade erupted -- five hunters gleefully blasting away with their rifles. Three of the Undead took chest shots and reeled back but did not go down. Some of the others were shot in the head and fell heavily to the ground.

Stush yelled, "Don't hit the girl, for chrissake! I don't want her dead!"

The men -- and one woman -- of the shooting party advanced toward the surviving zombies. The depraved hunters were slavering at the prospect of slaying something human-like instead of shooting at "lower animals" or, worse, stationary targets in the shape of a man.

(This kind of behavior is exactly why Mark Twain called man "the only animal that blushes, or needs to.)

The hunters blasted away till all the zombies were slain. Then they started arguing over the kills while Betty kept bleeding and whimpering with ghouls lying dead all around her.

Joe Talerico, one of the creeps who had captured her, proudly said, "I shot the old dude in the vest! Mark *me* up for that one, Stush!" He was wearing his deer-hunting clothes: an orange ball cap and a padded woodsman's outfit with reflective orange bands on it.

Stush was sitting at a card table with a ballpoint pen, a cash box full of money, and a revolver close at hand. His face was jowly and seamed, his black eyes perpetually wary. At the camp he always wore worn-out jeans, a black turtleneck, a tattered denim jacket with tarnished brass buttons, and a black slouch hat. He stopped with his pen in midair when the female hunter, a beautiful brunette wearing an Australian bush hat and amber shooting glasses, piped up angrily, "That was *my* kill, not yours, Joe! You men act like you're the *only* ones who know how to shoot!"

Joe said, "Bite me, Judy!"

"I didn't see who shot first," Stush said, "so I'll give each of you *half* a kill."

A hunter named Sam said, "I got one, Stush. Don't try to cheat me out of it!"

His brother Hal backed him up. "I vouch for that. Mark it down, Stush." Sam and Hal were each wearing olive-drab jumpsuits, red neckerchiefs and red ball caps -- rough-looking men with thick black beards, not even shaved around the neck, who looked so much alike they could have passed as twins even though Hal was a couple years older.

"I had two kills," Hal said gruffly, "and I want full credit for them, Stush."

A guy named Pete, clad in denims and scuffed-up cowboy boots, said, "My two kills were clean head shots. Don't try to say you guys didn't see that."

But Dan Lancaster, who had helped Joe Talerico kidnap Betty, snarlingly said, "You're the biggest bullshitter in the world, Pete. When you go deer hunting you always claim you bagged a ten-pointer. But I never see any heads hanging on your wall, do I?"

The other hunters all guffawed at this, and Pete said, "You can all go fuck yourselves."

Stush said, "All right, Pete. I agree you got two today. That brings your total to thirty-

seven for the summer. Joe and Judy, you each bagged three. Your scores are tied at twenty-two apiece."

Pete emitted a barking laugh and took a swig of vodka from a shiny metal flask. "You guys'll never catch me! Might as well give me the kitty right now! How much is in it, Stush?"

"Two-thousand bucks."

"Great! Two months mortgage!"

Dan said, "Don't gloat, motherfucker!"

"Don't fucking argue," Stush said. "You guys gotta burn the bodies and cage the girl. We gotta keep Betty alive 'cause she's gonna turn into one of 'em, and she can make us more every time we let her bite on someone."

"Why do all the victims have to be girls?" Judy complained. "You guys are a bunch of fucking chauvinists!"

"I'm not a chauvinist in bed," said Dan. "I *give* as many orgasms as I *get*. Wanna try me, Judy?"

"My bar ain't that low!" Judy snapped.

"I'd be the best you ever had," Dan bragged.

"Better than the hairy asses you had in prison?" Judy taunted.

Dan stomped away muttering to Joe under his breath. "Someday I'm gonna kill that bitch. Or else set her up so she gets bit by a zombie."

"That I'd like to see," Joe said, snickering. "Then we could hunt her down and shoot her."

CHAPTER 7

The Rave and the Crazy Preacher

Cy-Fi rented a theater for a Tuesday night, a slow night for movies, when she could get it cheap enough for her budget. She was going to throw a rave and a fashion show for the Goth outfits and jewelry that she sold at her store, and she had fliers made up advertising that I would be there. She figured I was getting famous enough to help draw a crowd. The fashion show was first on the bill because she wanted it to happen before everybody got all doped and liquored up.

A half dozen of her models were all decked out in fancy high-end corsets, gowns and lingerie. The stage was all lit up with multicolored pulsing strobes and the huge backdrop was a collage of grisly scenes from famous horror movies. The audience was gathered in the shadowy seating area of the theater, drinking, whistling and laughing as the girls strutted their stuff.

My nephew Oscar was stationed near the stage wearing his security guard uniform, his hand on the butt of his holstered pistol, prepared for any kind of trouble. I didn't feel all that comforted by his presence. Any person there could be carrying a concealed weapon in a purse or under a shirt. I knew full well that law and order was brought to the Wild West only when vigilantes started hanging outlaws in their cells and sheriffs started making desperadoes check their guns on the outskirts of town. Once again we have learned no lessons from our past and have brought the Wild West into our towns and cities. And I had to be more worried about this than most people because I had become a minor celebrity.

I sat in the front row, near the stage and near Oscar. I hoped his mind wouldn't wander in the presence of the lovely models. As the first one strutted out from among the bevy of six, Cy-Fi announced her over the microphone and P.A. system. "Let's have a big hand for Kat! Isn't she gorgeous? She's wearing one of our top-of-the-line Victorian gowns, complete with a low-cut bodice and a bustle."

The audience applauded and made cat-calls, and I tried to clap but my hands were a bit stiffer than usual because I was over-anxious. I turned around to see if anybody with malicious intent might have his or her eyes on me, and that's when I spotted Detective Jane Smart close by, in an alcove, eyeing the goings-on piercingly. As if she felt me staring at her, she focused on me with what I felt to be a deadly glower.

She wasn't the worst danger that was near to me that night. I didn't know it, but we were being picketed right outside the theater. Under a bright streetlamp, about thirty or forty people were gathered around a fanatical preacher, chanting and carrying signs. Later, when I saw them on television, they reminded me of the nut cases who picket soldiers' funerals or abortion clinics, but instead of signs like GOD HATES GAYS! or ABORTIONISTS MUST DIE! their signs trumpeted THE DEAD MUST BE SPIKED! or ZOMBIES ARE SATAN'S MINIONS!

They were all caught up in mob psychology; in other words, a dangerous hysteria.

The preacher's name was Reverend Hotchkiss, and he was wearing a black suit and a Roman collar, and he had wild, flowing white hair. In his right hand he clutched a large wooden homemade cross whittled to a sharp point. He led his followers in their chant, waving his arms in a crazed rhythm like an enraged choir director. SPIKE THE DEAD! SPIKE THE DEAD! ZOMBIES LOVE SATAN! SPIKE THE DEAD! SPIKE THE DEAD! SPIKE THE DEAD!

Oblivious to all this, inside the theater Cy-Fi's show still went on. When the parade of models in gaudy clothing was finished to great applause, she launched into her spiel for a fire-breathing demonstration. "As you all know, I'm a wiccan, and some people think wiccans are evil witches or something. But nothing could be farther from the truth."

Detective Jane Smart by now had moved so close to me that I heard her derisive snort as she shook her head in disbelief and glared at Cy-Fi with looks that could kill.

Unaware of this, I think, Cy-Fi went on. "Wiccans believe that by communing with the highly spiritual forces in nature we can achieve communion with these forces -- call them the Great Spirit, or God, if you will. This is the key to pacifying your soul and mastering special powers like the breathing of fire, which I am now going to demonstrate. Uncle John is still afraid of fire, and with good reason, as we all know. Oscar, will you escort him a little further from the stage, please?"

Cy-Fi's models were sitting in the front row with me now, and two of them got up and helped me to my feet, and Oscar took me by the arm and led me to a farther corner. On the way we brushed past Detective Smart, which made me more than a little uncomfortable.

As soon as I was at a safe distance, Cy-Fi exhaled an eight-foot blast of flame from her mouth! It was something I always hated to see -- but the audience erupted in wild applause, whistles and hoots. They were absolutely delighted, but Jane Smart eyed Cy-Fi derisively.

I cowered back from the bright flames and got behind Oscar even though I was at least ten feet back from the stage.

Meanwhile, out in the street, Steve Munch and Mandy Frost had pulled up in a FLSH-TV van and she was interviewing Reverend Hotchkiss with his fanatical followers gathered tightly around him. Hotchkiss was still clutching his spiked cross.

Into her microphone Mandy said, "Good evening, Reverend Hotchkiss, I'm Mandy Frost from FLSH-TV. Why do you think we still have to drive spikes into the heads of dead people?"

"Zombies are not human any longer!" Hotchkiss shrieked. "They are soulless creatures! They must be spiked so they can die and go to Purgatory! Otherwise they will continue to spread their sickening satanic illness! They've made their intentions perfectly clear again and again. The zombie plague is God's way of punishing us for our sins!"

"Punishing everybody?" Mandy said. "Even little children?"

"Children are not perfectly innocent," said Hotchkiss. "They are the embodiment of sins just waiting to happen. It's just a matter of time. They share the original sin of Adam and Eve."

"So you and your followers believe that dead people must have those spiked crosses driven into their heads? Even though the zombie disease seems to be under control these days? Like cholera or diphtheria."

"It's not under control! How can you say that, Mandy? It's still dangerous to stop vaccinating against the diseases you mentioned, just because we believe we're safe. A zombie epidemic can break out at any time! God wants us to spike the dead! Any sane person has to believe that. I used to preach against the gay and lesbian lifestyle, but the zombie lifestyle is far worse. God called on me to focus my ministry on zombies instead of gays."

With an appalled look on her face, Mandy said, "Reverend Hotchkiss, what do you have to say about my interview with Cy-Fi and Uncle John? It's clear that many people are intrigued by them."

"They must be spiked! Both of them! They are minions of Satan!"

"But she seems to be a nice young woman with good intentions that are a bit misguided. She just wants to help her uncle. She might not be completely stable, mentally, but surely she needs to be treated, not killed, wouldn't you say?"

"Well, the Lord commands us to be merciful, but he also commands us to be obedient," Hotchkiss said adamantly. "We are charged with carrying out His work here on earth. That's why we must put aside any troubling leanings toward mercy. We had to do things that same way back in the Dark Ages when we were called upon to burn millions of witches at the stake. We knew they were worshiping Satan! They were enemies of the Lord!"

"But many of them were innocent, weren't they? Yet they were tortured and made to confess."

"A few honest mistakes were made," Hotchkiss said with a derisive snort. "But the inquisitors had their hearts in the right place."

"I'm not so sure about that," said Mandy.

By the time I had left the theater with Oscar, Hotchkiss and his crowd of picketers were no longer on the sidewalk, so I didn't know about him till I saw the news the next day. Cy-Fi's show had ended too, and her crowd had dissipated, and it was then that Jane Smart came forward to interrogate her, first cajolingly her by saying, "I must admit you put on quite a show."

"Thank you, detective," Cy-Fi said, on guard against the flattery.

Jane plunged right in. "I need you to answer some questions. I want to interview *you*, your brother *and* your uncle -- separately."

"Oscar took Uncle John home and put him to bed," Cy-Fi countered. "It was a long day for him and he needs his rest. Why would you want to talk to him anyhow? After all, he's not a criminal."

"Oh, he isn't? And *you're* not? I'm betting you know all the grisly details about the murder I'm investigating -- even the ones we held back."

"I seldom watch the news," Cy-Fi parried. "So I don't know what you're talking about."

"You don't know about the child molester, Clyde Yancey, who was found murdered?"

"No, but it couldn't have happened to a nicer guy."

"Did you have anything to do with it, Cy-Fi? Or your brother Oscar? Or your Uncle John?"

"Why would we go after a child molester? That's *your* job, isn't it? You're the *cop*, not us."

"I saw you on the air. I reviewed the tape, looked at it a number of times as a matter of fact. You told Mandy Frost that your uncle needs to eat, and you let slip how you choose his diet. You implied that you select people you think the world would be better off without."

"What if everything I said was just a big put-on? What if I'm not serious about any of it, and what if Uncle John isn't really a zombie?"

"Well, we didn't find Yancey's right forearm at the crime scene."

"You think Uncle John ate it? And I fed it to him or something?"

"I have a hunch that's how it went down -- no pun intended. I wonder if you even cooked it for him -- with those flames you spew out."

Cy-Fi couldn't help laughing. "That's so far-fetched, Detective! I thought cops are supposed to go on *evidence*, not hunches!"

"Correct," Jane squelched. "And if we find Uncle John's saliva on a partially eaten body part, we'll have his DNA, whether he's a real zombie or a fake. And we'll nail him. And you and Oscar along with him. One thing about prison food -- it won't be the kind he claims he needs!"

CHAPTER 8

An American Horror Story

I know full well that many people will say "Consider the source," as if I can't have anything cogent to say, just because I'm a zombie. But I haven't lost touch with what's going on in the world, even though I might have one foot in the grave or *two* feet *out* of the grave, I don't know which. Along with my speech faculty, I still retain my interest in the arts, the humanities and politics.

When I was a college professor, I wrote a book entitled *The Death of Our Democracy: An American Horror Story.* It was a collection of essays on American history and culture, a mirror into my mind, so to speak. Luckily, my mind remains less damaged than other parts of me. I worry about the way the country is going, which is mostly in the wrong direction.

The earth is a Ship of Fools hurtling us through space while we shit in our own nest. We fill the sky with pollution and the oceans with plastic bags. We humans are overpopulating the earth like a horde of hungry locusts -- no way can our planet support eight billion people and climbing. We badly need population control and climate control. We need a political system that works for all of us, and we need to understand it, believe in it and fully take part in it.

In the Golden Age of Athenian democracy, Pericles said, "We do not say that a man who takes no interest in politics minds his own business; we say that he has no business here at all." His words call out to us today, urging us to participate. But it seems most people take no interest in anything but fiddling with their Smart Phones.

When Benjamin Franklin was asked what the Constitutional Convention had bestowed upon us, he said, "A republic, madam, if you can keep it." But I fear we are in danger of losing it. Losing to the oligarchs, the lobbyists and the autocrats.

H.L. Mencken said, "As democracy is perfected, the office of president represents, more and more closely, the inner soul of the people. On some great and glorious day, the plain folks of the land will reach their heart's desire at last and the White House will be adorned by a downright moron."

Our present Commander in Chief was actually *called* a moron by his own Secretary of State. But I don't think he's unintelligent, just arrogant, power mad and narcissistic. He doesn't understand the Constitution or the Separation of Powers. He tries to run the country as if he's the boss, a dictator in his own mind. He conjures up, not our "better angels," as Abraham Lincoln put it, but our worst inner demons. He turns us against each other. He's not just against illegal immigrants but *all* immigrants. His heavy-handed policies have the fervent support of a conglomeration of neo-fascist groups who feel that he is tacitly on their side. They even dare to openly give him the Nazi salute at his rabble-rousing rallies.

During the first zombie outbreak back in 1968 there was no such thing as the Department of Homeland Security. Local, state and federal law agencies banded together with armed citizens to bring things under control. But nowadays our President is able to make use of not just the Department of Homeland Security (a title that always did sound Nazi-like to me) but also the Immigration and Naturalization Service (ICE). He's in the process of deporting over 800,000 children who have known no other home but the United States after being brought in by parents who came here illegally. He insists that we must build a wall to try to keep out Mexicans. And

he keeps trying to totally ban people from Muslim countries because he thinks they're all nascent terrorists. He whips up his 36-million-strong voter-base so they'll keep on supporting him and making decent people afraid to start any legal proceedings against him, such as impeachment, because his legion of rabid followers would almost certainly plunge us into outright rebellion and anarchy.

As a famous cartoon strip once pointed out, "The enemy is us." We kill forty thousand of our fellow citizens every year with firearms, ten times as many as were ever killed by terrorists. Over the past five decades, about two million people have been killed by *people with guns* but only about two-hundred-thousand by *zombies!* Yet the zombies are feared more than the people with guns. And the zombies don't do it maliciously, all they're trying to do is get something to eat. But our President, in his infinite wisdom, has recently signed an Executive Order making it perfectly legal to *shoot* zombies even if we weren't caught taking a bite out of *anyone*. No arrest, no trial, no habeas corpus, just execution on sight.

Luckily we have "sanctuary cities" -- compassionate refuges for immigrants and zombies. Many people don't approve of mindless deportation or slaughter of these poor folks. But I think that the President would like to put all the immigrants into concentration camps and heave all the zombies onto bonfires. But for now, public sentiment holds him back.

I hope you will be moved by what I am saying and not pooh-pooh me just because I'm a zombie. My ghostwriter, John Russo, has been encouraging me to start a web site, a podcast and a Face Book page to help me get my message across and sell books. He even thinks that *my* book, *An American Horror Story*, can furnish a wealth of material for blogs. He said that after I accumulate enough followers we can have Cy-Fi and Oscar on my podcast as featured guests, and we should even be able to land interviews with other fascinating and controversial people. I'm really looking forward to it. It will be a bully pulpit, much more exciting and I hope with a far greater impact than I had when I was a professor haranguing kids in my classroom and trying in vain to keep them from falling asleep. They didn't want to hear my lectures. They couldn't wait to get back to fiddling with their smartphones.

CHAPTER 9

The Zombie Acting Academy

Jane Smart was so bent on proving that I was a fake that she actually went to a fly-by-night place calling itself a Zombie Acting Academy. She thought I might be there taking lessons -- but of course I didn't need any.

As soon as Jane stepped through the door, about a dozen zombies came at her, rasping and drooling. She almost passed out, fainted, from sheer shock, which would have definitely been rather unbecoming for a police officer. But the reason was that she had tossed and turned all night, bathed in sweat, having one of her recurrent nightmares about having to shoot her own mother who was coming at her as a zombie.

She jumped back, woozy, sagging against a wall, fighting to recover herself. Everybody in the room stared at her, which included all the zombies and the purported "zombie acting coach" -- a mousey little twerp named Herb Bonnet.

Jane managed to pull out her badge and her gun and yelled, "Back off! Get away from me or I'll blast you!"

Herb Bonnet said, "No! Don't shoot! They're harmless!"

Jane eyed him piercingly, her face full of fear and doubt. "You better control them!" she said, "if you don't want to be dragged out of here in handcuffs!"

"But they're harmless," he pleaded. "They're just here to learn how to act in the movies."

"I'll stand back and watch," said Jane. "But if they make one false move I'll shoot!"

Frantically, the coach urged the class of about thirteen zombies to take their seats. The place had posters of zombie movies on the wall, most of which were of films made by John Russo and George Romero. And the room was set up like a standard classroom, with seats and desks.

When the zombies were all seated again the coach said, "Now, everybody pay close attention. I'm going to demonstrate how zombies are supposed to look and sound when they're on screen. Remember, most people have gotten used to the concept, popularized by Romero and others, that every zombie has a certain amount of rigor mortis. So, watch me -- this is the way you must move on-camera."

He shambled around the room for a long while, moaning and hissing, looking half paralytic, while his zombie students looked on, and so did Jane Smart, who shook her head in disgust and disbelief.

Finally Herb Bonnet straightened up behind a podium and said, "There! I hope all of you paid close attention. Any questions?"

A young male zombie put his hand up. He was wearing bibbed coveralls, a plaid shirt and yellow clodhoppers, so Jane thought he probably was a farmer at one time, and maybe still.

"Yes, William?" Herb Bonnet said, obviously pleased to be getting a response from one of his students. (I must confess I know the feeling.)

William said, "I don't really have rigor mortis anymore. I only had it for a few days, then it went away after I had my first taste of human flesh. So, am I supposed to fake it, just because some movie director wants it that way?"

"If you don't give the director exactly what he wants, you won't get cast," the coach said. "So it's up to you how badly you want to land a good-paying gig and get your union card."

Union card? Jane thought. This crazy bastard can't be serious!

A female zombie put her hand up. Her dark hair was a tangled mess and she was wearing what probably used to be a nice housedress, but now it was torn and filthy. Her face was torn, too -- gaping blood-dried wounds on her forehead and both cheeks. Her arms were ghastly looking, too; it looked like chunks had been bitten out of them.

"Yes, Maria?" the coach said.

"What if I get cast in one of those slow-moving zombie movies where they want the zombies to be able to run?" Maria asked. Her voice was a slow, pain-filled slur, almost convincing Jane that she was a real zombie. "I'm really dead, so I can't run fast, and I can't crack anybody's skull open and eat his brains -- unless the skull's already cracked open in an accident or a murder or something."

"You won't have to worry about that," the coach answered with assurance. "If they need fast zombies, they'll cast experienced actors. And if the script calls for the kind who eat brains, they'll have the prop department make fake brains and fake skulls that open up easily."

Maria nodded her head and sort of smiled as much as she could, obviously feeling much better about her prospects.

"Now let's move on with our exercise," Herb Bonnet said. "Let me see you all do the zombie walk like I did. One...two...three...go!"

The so-called acting class started shambling around, imitating the walk that the coach already demonstrated -- and Jane stepped up and got right in his face. "Listen, Mister Zombie Acting Coach -- you're perpetrating a fraud here, and I'm going to bring you down and put you behind bars!"

"You have no grounds for prosecuting me!" the coach shot back. "These people want to learn, and I'm here to teach them. I'm not committing any crime here."

"How much are they paying you?"

"A hundred dollars apiece per session."

"That's disgusting! Apparently they believe they're zombies, and you're defrauding them, taking advantage of their sick delusions. I'll need their names and addresses. I'm going to persuade them to file a class action suit against you."

"But all they want to do is get into a John Russo movie or a *Walking Dead* episode, and I'm helping them!"

"You're nothing but a con man," Jane spat. "That movie *Night of the Living Dead* started it all -- and now there are Zombie Walks, zombie yoga classes, zombie speech therapists and zombie employment agencies. It's appalling!"

Herb Bonnet said, "Good-paying jobs are hard to get these days, and the Republican so-called tax reform hurt the poor and the middle class. These zombies have to find some way of earning a living while they're hoping and praying for a cure."

"Well, I feel sorry for them," Jane said. "But if I catch any of them chomping on somebody it'll be their last bite of human flesh."

She stomped out of the Zombie Acting Academy, disappointed that she didn't find me there and all the more convinced that she was on the right track by suspecting me and Oscar and Cy-Fi of having a hand in the shooting and partial butchering of Clyde Yancey.

CHAPTER 10

My First Podcast

This was an exciting day for me, that's for sure! We decided to run my first podcast on a Tuesday night, when people would not have lots of other things to do like going to parties, sports events and movies. For weeks in advance, my Face Book page and my web site were on fire with queries and comments anticipating the big event. I was flattered and amazed at all the fuss and furor I had caused.

We agreed that John Russo and I would be co-hosts. Since we wanted all of our podcasts to be issue-oriented instead of just purely entertaining, we intended to start off talking about the health care debate that had been raging on and on for more than a decade. We knew that the outcome was vital not just to millions of *non*-infected people, but also to all the other zombies out there, the ones still in hiding and the ones who had already come out, only to be persecuted or shot down.

I also badly wanted to speak out against the latest Executive Order from the President that was so terribly hazardous for all of us who were Undead. We had already launched a petition on the Internet, and I wanted to get millions of signatures if I could.

Here is a partial transcript of our very first podcast. **UJ** is me and **JR** stands for John Russo. I led into the discussion with a rap that I thought would instigate follow-up tweets and blogs. I even hoped that the President would tweet something because he was known not to be able to stop himself from tweeting, no matter how nonsensical, inaccurate or hateful that some of his tweets were.

UJ: Welcome, everybody, to Uncle John's first podcast. I'm Uncle John and I thank you for logging on. I hope you will continue to log on every chance you get. We need your support. The Republican-dominated Congress keeps trying to repeal and replace the Affordable Care Act, otherwise known as Obama Care. But their kind of care is equal to no care at all for the poor and the middle class. We're the only advanced nation that doesn't have a single-payer universal health care system. It's time we stopped lagging behind.

JR: Some people are going to say that you have far too much of a vested interest in this. How do you respond, Uncle John?

UJ: Well, of course I do. All American citizens do, especially us zombies. I'm living proof that the zombie disease doesn't need to be a death sentence. I can still enjoy my life and do many normal things. I still have my speech faculty. If I can survive and thrive, so can many others. We have to step up our effort to find a total cure.

JR: In the meantime, would you support a quarantine?

UJ: That would be preferable to driving spikes in our heads or gunning us down and cremating us or bulldozing us into trenches.

JR: As you know, George Romero and I wrote the screenplay for *Night of the Living Dead*. It's considered a classic motion picture. Honors have been heaped upon it, including a brand new state-of-the-art restoration by the Museum of Modern Art. How has that movie affected you?

UJ: With all due respect, Mr. Russo, there wasn't much nuance in that movie where us zombies were concerned. You portrayed us as evil, two-dimensional, cannibalistic brutes driven solely by our cravings for human flesh. You forgot all about our humanity. You didn't bother to explore our back stories to any extent at all. Your audiences learned virtually nothing about us -- our dreams, our aspirations, our jobs, our friendships, our family relationships, our contributions to society before we got infected.

JR: I have to admit that's a fair criticism.

UJ: It made people all too willing to destroy us without feeling any pangs of conscience whatsoever. We're suffering to this day from the unsympathetic stereotype you created.

JR: Again, that's a fair criticism. I have to apologize. You've lambasted the President and the Congress for a wide range of failings, especially their insensitivity to people's health care needs and the plight of zombies. What do you think the solution is?

UJ: We have to get the money out of politics. We need public financing of election campaigns, and we badly need term limits.

JR: Why?

UJ: Well, I must tell you that when I was a college professor I used to teach my students the advantages of *not* having term limits. I used to say that because our congressmen could stay in office long enough to form friendships and alliances with one another, enough common ground could be established to make the wheels of government turn more efficiently and not get bogged down. But the unintended consequence is that our two-party system has become so tribal that Congress is completely gridlocked. They achieve absolutely nothing for the people they are supposed to be working for. All they care about is getting reelected and hanging onto their fat salaries, perks and pensions. They spend all their time raising money so they can keep feeding from the public trough. They're totally beholden to the billionaires and the major corporations who keep giving them fat donations.

JR: How would term limits help?

UJ: Well, if they were only in for a term or two, maybe they'd grow some balls. And with public financing they wouldn't have to kiss the donors' asses.

JR: That makes sense. It sounds like stuff you said in your book, *The Death of Our Democracy: An American Horror Story.* I heartily recommend it to our listeners. You offered some highly penetrating insights before you became a zombie.

UJ: I'm still offering them, don't forget. If only people will listen!

JR: Yes, you still have an alert mind, Uncle John. I've been happy to find that out. Let's take some calls from our listeners.

To my surprise, the first call was from my niece, Cy-Fi. She must've been listening at home on her computer. I had told her that John Russo and I wanted to handle the first podcast on our own and I promised we'd have her as a guest on the second one, but she was too impetuous to wait. I should've known she'd be irrepressible.

She said, "I want to announce that my brother Oscar and I, who have kept Uncle John alive all these years, have now formed an advocacy group called the Zombie Protection Society, ZPS. Oscar is on this call with me, on another line. We want to help Uncle John call attention to the plight of zombies everywhere. Even as I speak, they're being abused and mistreated. Zombie hunting camps actually exist, far from prying eyes, where unscrupulous people pay big money to hunt them and kill them as if they're unfeeling targets in a shooting gallery."

Oscar chimed in, saying, "My sister and I believe in the humane treatment of all people, even the unlucky ones who have come down with the same disease Uncle John has."

Cy-Fi said, "We want to assure you that zombies can continue to be lovable family members in spite of their illness. They are naturally a little slow and inept, but most of them can perform valuable household chores like mowing grass and pruning hedges."

"Yeah," said Oscar. "Some of them can even be taught to wash and dry dishes without breaking them."

"That's why we've formed GPS," Cy-Fi enthused. "The Zombie Protection Society! Please join us in our humanitarian crusade. You can pay our modest membership fee, only $19.68. Download your own personal membership certificate or get it in the mail by going to our web site, myunclejohnisazombie.com or by phoning 1-800-ZOMBIES."

John Russo and I thanked them, and they got off the line to make way for other callers.

Unfortunately, the very next call was from Reverend Ebenezer Hotchkiss, the fanatic who wanted to drive a spiked cross into my head. In a shrill, hysterical voice that belied his so-called Holy Calling, he announced himself. "I'm the pastor of The Church of Lazarus Risen," he said, "and I speak for Our Lord Jesus Christ! Zombies must be spiked!"

John Russo remained much calmer than I did. In even and well-modulated tones, he said, "Thanks for your call, Reverend. This is an open forum." All you've opened is the Gates of Hell!" the preacher shrieked. "I'm coming for Uncle John! And I have the Lord's blessing! Mine is the Power of the Holy Ghost! And I will gird my loins and do Jehovah's work! The dead must be spiked! And I will do so! In the Name of the Father, the Son and the Holy Spirit!"

"Hmph! What makes you so smug you think that you speak for God?" I asked him.

But he started chanting "Spike the dead!" over and over.

We finally cut him off. But I admit he had me shaken. I figured that everywhere I went I'd have to be constantly looking over my shoulder, wondering when he was going to come charging at me with that spiked cross of his.

CHAPTER 11

I Submit to Medical Tests

I felt so insulted that a lot of people were taking me for a liar that I finally went for a complete physical exam. Yippee! The tests confirmed my claims! And Mandy Frost announced the results on FLSH-TV:

"Bombshell, everybody! Uncle John, the zombie I made famous, has submitted to a battery of tests conducted at the Zombie Research Institute in Evans City, Pennsylvania. This ought to settle once and for all the issue of whether or not Uncle John is a bona fide flesh-eating zombie! We have an on-camera report from Dr. Delbert Strange, the head of the venerable, highly respected Institute."

Dr. Strange, a bespectacled eccentric with hair like Albert Einstein's, came onto the broadcast. "Uncle John's blood pressure is nonexistent, and his body is always at room temperature. He has no blood circulation, his vital fluids are coagulated in his veins and arteries. But his brain and nervous system are almost fully functioning; in other words his brain seems normal, but his nerves are somewhat impaired, giving him that zombie-like gait. It seems, amazingly, that he retains a sex urge and an ability. This is what we see in some patients whose necks have been broken, disabling movement from the neck down. Yet they can still get erections, because that mechanism is operated by a different part of the nervous system."

"Operated independently?" Mandy asked Dr. Strange.

"Yes. I believe that we here at the Zombie Research Institute have made a breakthrough discovery about how certain people become reanimated even though they are dead."

"Stay tuned to this program for updates on this remarkable story!" Mandy said, glowing excitedly. "It seems we can be sure that Uncle John is actually a walking, talking, flesh-eating corpse!"

I felt vindicated. It heartened me to know that, because of my podcast and the results of my physical, people were realizing that I still retained a great deal of vitality and a wry, witty sense of humor. I found it especially gratifying that Dr. Strange had openly stated that, in spite of my infirmities, I possessed a healthy, if unrequited, sex appetite.

After the results of that exam were announced, my popularity started to spread faster than the zombie apocalypse itself. I had my podcast going, but I was also a popular guest on lots of television shows -- and not just the news programs. I even got hired as a spokesperson for a beer called Cold Crypt Pilsner and a sexual aid called Uncle John's Zombie Lube, developed by me and Dr. Strange, because he urged me to do it after he got to know me. I came up with the catch-line used when I appeared in the TV spots for it: *It'll give a stiff a stiffy, so imagine what it'll do for you!!*

The downside to all this was that I couldn't go anywhere without being recognized. And surprisingly enough, certain kinds of women even came on to me. But Cy-Fi wouldn't let me hook up with them. She distrusted their motives, now that I was becoming affluent. She didn't out-and-out call them gold diggers, but I could tell that's what she thought.

There were people who were jealous of me, too -- especially movie characters and comic book heroes who had been big stars and now felt they were losing popularity because of me. Sgt. Kabuki Man and The Toxic Avenger, made famous by Troma Films, had many movies and tie-in products on the market, and they despised the fact that I was making more money than they were and winning over their fans. They resented that the public now thought I was for real and they weren't. This put me in greater danger than I was in before. Troma's president, Lloyd Kaufman, got in touch with Stush Polanski and the two of them started hatching an evil plot against me, even as I was basking in my newfound success.

Lloyd showed up at Stush's camp one day just as Stush was teaching his grandkids how to shoot zombies. The boy was nine and the girl was eleven, and he had bought them each a pink child-sized .22 rifle for Christmas. One of his hunters, Joe Talerico, the same guy who took part in the kidnapping of Betty Montgomery, was tying a father and his daughter, both zombies, to a stake, and even Joe had qualms about it. "You're gonna let your grandkids shoot this little girl?" he asked quizzically.

"That's pretty cold," Lloyd agreed.

"Yeah, they're us and we're them," Joe said, quoting a line from a Romero film.

Stush said, "Bullshit! They're not us and we're not them! They're fuckin' monsters and there ain't nothin' wrong with blastin' 'em in the head!"

His grandson said, "I wanna shoot them, Grandpa!"

And his granddaughter said, "Me, too!"

"These kids was raised right! They know the second amendment backwards and forwards," Stush boasted. "Tell 'em, kids!"

The boy shouted, "I have a right to bear arms!"

And the girl shouted, "I'll give up my gun when they pry it from my cold dead hands!"

"Chips off the old block!" Stush said. "What'd I tell ya?"

"Okay, ready!" Joe called out, and hurried to get twenty feet away from the kids' tied-up targets because he didn't trust their aim.

Stush said, "Do like I told ya, kids! Sight in on 'em nice and steady, then squeeze the trigger, don't jerk it."

Lloyd Kaufman squeamishly shut his eyes and turned his head.

Bang!

Bang!

Bang!

And when Lloyd dared to look again, both zombies, the man and his young daughter, had bloody holes in their heads and were as limp as rag dolls.

Lloyd wondered with great anxiety what he was getting into with this depraved guy he had hooked up with by the name of Stush Polanski. But he had to use Stush to get rid of Uncle John. On his plane ride back to New York City, he worried about it all the way. He even thought of calling the whole thing off.

However, Stush had no such pangs of conscience. That same day, after Lloyd was gone, he and Joe Talerico and Dan Lancaster dragged a tied-up young woman toward the zombie cage as she struggled vainly to get away from them and pleaded for her life. "Please...let me *go!* I won't tell anybody! *Please!"*

Stush said, "Sorry, but I can't take that chance, honey buns."

"Let me *go!* You can *trust* me, I promise!"

"Too late, babe. They're hungry for you. You smell delicious to them."

He meant the zombies in the cage. It was made of thick chain-linked steel, and it was being banged and rattled by starving zombies making a hell of a racket. There were presently about ten of them, including Betty, the voluptuous miss in a yellow bikini who was previously staked out as a lure. Now she was going to have her first bite of human flesh.

Unlocking the cage door, Stush said to Joe and Dan, "Use those ten-foot bamboos! Push 'em *back* so they can't bite *us!"*

Joe and Dan grabbed the poles and prodded the rasping and growling zombies to the back of the cage. Then they jumped back and dragged the struggling fear-ridden victim inside, and Stush slammed and locked the door.

The zombies shambled hungrily forward, toward the struggling, screaming girl.

Betty got to her first.

Then the others closed in.

CHAPTER 12

The Preacher's Attack

On the day that the bad thing happened, Oscar and I had finished a hot, sweaty jog through the park, and were sitting on a bench licking ice cream cones.

The previous night, Reverend Hotchkiss had knelt at the side of his bed, praying, and very distressed. We didn't know it at the time, but he was thinking about doing me in, and he thought it was God's will and he was committing a mortal sin by putting it off. Near him on the unmade bed was his big cross-shaped spike, which had made himself, carving it by hand from a hunk of hickory: a very efficient, scary-looking weapon.

"Have mercy on me, Lord," he prayed fervently. "And guide me in Thy infinite wisdom so I can see the Light and do the right thing. I want nothing more than to do Thy bidding! But I am a humble mortal, Lord, and I am not always given to see the Light. I believe that I must vanquish the minions of Satan, Cy-Fi, Oscar and Uncle John, and I am looking for a Heavenly Sign that you will aid me in doing Thy will! I earnestly pray for the Power of the Holy Ghost to descend upon me and to give me strength in Thy Holy Mission! Amen!"

As luck would have it (for I don't believe in miracles even though some might call *me* one), the minute Hotchkiss said "Amen" a bolt of lightning shattered the sky outside his window and lit up his bedroom for several long, overpowering seconds. As a matter of fact, the light show struck three times in succession, which to him seemed totally ominous. He covered his face with his hands and wept copiously, overcome with religious emotion. Then he gazed upward with beatific awe in his eyes and shouted, "Thank you for the Sign from Heaven, dear Lord! Now I will gird my loins and summon all my courage to do Thy bidding!"

So saying, he took his spiked cross in both his hands and reverently kissed it.

This is what Oscar and I were up against. But we didn't yet know it that bright, sunny day in the park.

It might surprise you that I like ice cream. But I do enjoy all types of food, not just human flesh, although I must definitely consume that now and then.   It being zombie's only sustenance is a fiction perpetrated by books and movies.

Jokingly, Oscar said, "Aren't you gonna hurt your tummy, Uncle John? You're not really s'posed to be eatin' nothin' but fresh meat."

I chuckled along with him, knowing he was joking about the popular myth.

I said, "You know I love ice cream, Oscar. I used to buy cones for you and Cy-Fi when you were little kids."

"Yeah," Oscar said, licking his lips. "She even told that to that reporter -- Mandy Frost, the hot little number from FLSH-TV."

"I remember her," said I. "I'd like to lick *her!*"

Oscar chuckled, then straightened himself up, saying, "Good thing Cy-Fi ain't here. She don't like to hear you talk dirty."

"There's nothing dirty about sex, Oscar. I wish I'd have gotten a lot more of it before I turned into *this*."

"You're an okay dude in my book. I'm proud to be your nephew. Especially now that you're such a star on TV. I just worry that the wrong kinda people might come after you, Uncle John."

"Like who?"

"Like Reverend Hotchkiss, that crazy preacher. I think he has it in for you. Cy-Fi says he's an out-and-out bible thumper and he hates our kind of lifestyle. Especially yours."

"I can't help it. I didn't make myself this way. I don't know *what* made me this way!"

Oscar said, "That preacher blames it on the devil."

"Well, that's what all the bible thumpers always say when something they don't like is going on -- like the things their religion tells them not to eat that other people *like* to eat, or *have* to eat, or the things other people like to do in their own bedrooms."

"How's come you always make so much sense? You're kinda too deep for me to follow, but somehow you make me think you're mostly right and other people are wrong."

"They think I'm brain dead, but I'm not. The televangelists make me laugh. They act like they have a direct line to God and people believe them and make them rich."

`"That's for sure, Uncle John. They don't know as much as they think they do, or else why doesn't God tell them why you're like you are?" He thought for a moment, then said, "You better not tell Cy-Fi I let you have ice cream."

We gobbled up the last of our crunchy hard-cones, then Oscar took out a big red handkerchief and wiped off the dribbles that he got on his security guard uniform. He said, "Darn, Uncle John! How's come you're always neater than I am even though --" He realized he was about to say something that I might think insulting, so he broke it off. What he meant was that as stiff as I was from rigor mortis, I hadn't dripped any ice cream on my gray flannel jogging pants. It made him feel clumsy and inadequate compared to me, and he thought it shouldn't be that way. In his mind, why was I always so damned neat even though I looked so bad?

There were some kids on some swings in the field out past the gazebo, and I was bemused by them, watching them at play.

Oscar said, "Cute, ain't they?"

"Yeah, they bring back some happy memories of you and Cy-Fi when you were little. And even *farther* back when *I* was little. I started out in life pretty much like a normal kid. I even made good grades in Catholic grade school. But I did try to look up girls' dresses by scoping the reflections off of their shiny black shoes."

"Uncle John!" Oscar said chidingly. But then he got titillated enough to ask, "Did it work?"

"Nope. I only tried it because other kids bragged about getting beaver shots and jerking off thinking about it at night when they were in bed."

While we talked, we were totally unaware that Reverend Ebenezer Hotchkiss was lurking nearby with his cross-shaped spike. I guess he had been hiding in the bushes and ducking behind trees, stalking us while we were jogging, then he had sneaked up on us with nefarious intentions when we sat at the gazebo. Now he was stalking us again. But I imagine he didn't want to make his move while they were kids around. So he followed us as we began to stroll out of the park. When we lingered, he lingered. And when we resumed walking, he resumed too, brandishing his "holy implement for doing the Lord's work."

Finally, when we had our backs turned and had no idea he was behind us, he charged at

me with his sharpened cross raised high, yelling, "*Die!* You creature of *Satan!*"

At the last moment Oscar whirled and managed to grab the reverend's wrists. They wrestled mightily, tugging each other this way and that, while I backed off, jittery about the outcome.

Oscar punched the reverend in the stomach and he doubled over but he clung fanatically to his spiked cross. He pulled himself together and charged at me and I was too slow-moving to get out of his way. But Oscar grabbed him from behind just in time to save me, and again they were in a fight to the death.

Terrified, I backed away, then ran off and cowered behind a tree. I could peep out and watch, but they couldn't see me.

Oscar got Reverend Hotchkiss in a bear hug and started squeezing the breath out of him. But the reverend desperately clawed at Oscar's pistol, pulled it out of its holster and rammed the barrel into Oscar's gut.

Oscar fell down heavily near a sandbox -- and maybe he did this on purpose -- because while he was on his belly he surreptitiously grabbed a hand-full of sand. Then he pulled himself to his feet and warily eyed Reverend Hotchkiss.

The reverend had the upper hand -- he had the pistol in one hand and the spiked cross in the other, so he barked orders at Oscar. "*Now!* Where is he? Call him over here so I can spike him!"

Oscar said, "No way!"

"Do as I say!" Hotchkiss demanded. But when he jerkily glanced all around, trying to see where I could be hiding, Oscar flung a clump of sand in his face -- and he dropped the gun, his right hand went toward his eyes and he stumbled over the edge of the sandbox and fell on his face.

He hit the ground heavily, with a grunt, and lay still. Oscar shakily looked down at him, then rolled him over. I was still hiding, and I was badly shaken.

The reverend had fallen on his own spike. It was protruding from his chest, and he was dead. Maybe if he had a last thought it was to glory in what he would probably have thought of as martyrdom.

Oscar darted his eyes all around, looking for me. He picked up his gun and holstered it. Then he called out, "Uncle John? Uncle John! Where *are* you?"

I stepped slowly out from behind the tree. It was easy for Oscar to see that I was still scared.

"C'mon, he's not gonna hurt you anymore," Oscar said.

We both stood over the reverend's body, looking down at him. Some of the blood from the penetrating wound must have gone into his lungs but now it was leaking out of the corners of his mouth.

I ventured to say to Oscar, "Can I just...*you* know..."

"Nuh-uh," his said. I'd like to let you chew on some soft part of him, like maybe his belly, but..."

Holding out hope, I said, "We could pull his shirt up, then tuck it back in when I'm done."

"No, the cops'd come after us for sure. When they find his body, there's gonna be an autopsy, and we're so high on their radar right now, they're gonna come after *you*. Let's get the hell outta here, Uncle John!"

So I didn't get to eat. But the cops didn't find the body either. It happened that one of Stush's hunters, the one named Judy, had been tracking me, same as the reverend was, because Stush was interested in getting me alone so he could capture me. Judy had seen everything that transpired in the park, wearing a T-shirt and jeans, not her hunting garb.

She phoned Dan, telling him she needed help moving the body. "Bring your van," she said. "I'll come, but I don't have the van, Stush borrowed it. I'll have to get ahold of him."

In a short while, they were both standing over Reverend Hotchkiss's corpse, waiting for Stush, and Dan said, "Damn! He's right out in the open! I don't wanna get caught with my pants down."

"You have to take a crap?" Judy quipped.

"Very funny. We get caught with this stiff, we're gonna get hauled in."

"Why don't we drag him back in the bushes so the kids on the swings don't see him?"

"Sweet idea. Don't worry about messin' up his clothes. He's gonna be zombie feed anyways."

Judy said, "I can't help it, I hate to see a man of the cloth in his condition. I was raised to go to church every Sunday."

She blessed herself with the Sign of the Cross, an evil young woman but one who was still religious. Then she and Dan each grabbed one of Hotchkiss's ankles and dragged him over the grass and into a place obscured by wild bushes and tall, thick weeds. They dropped the ankles and looked around to see if anybody was watching, but nobody was.

Dan said to Judy, "Good thing you phoned me after what went down."

"Well, Stush told me to stick on Oscar and Uncle John in my spare time in case we could scavenge one of *their* meals for *our* zombies in the cage. Like, buzzards'll feast on what's left of a gazelle after the tiger that killed it is done eating."

"Yeah, Mother Nature is a great teacher," Dan said.

The both turned and looked when they heard the sound of an approaching vehicle, and Stush drove up in the van and jumped down from the driver's side. He spotted Dan and Judy as they stepped out from the bushes. "Where's the stiff?" he asked. "Let's load him up and get the hell outta here. Our zombies only like 'em fresh."

Dan said, "Right, boss. You open the back door to the van and me and Judy'll drag him over. He ain't gonna mind about grass stains -- heh-heh!"

After they got Hotchkiss's body loaded up, Dan extracted the spiked cross and wiped it on the grass, figuring to keep it for a souvenir.

Stush said, "Even though we didn't kill this jerk, we could still be charged for abuse of a corpse, so stop fuckin' around, Dan." He slammed the back door of the van shut, and they all got in and peeled out of there.

CHAPTER 13

Cy-Fi Appears on British TV

FLSH-TV obtained a tape of an interview with Cy-Fi that was shot by a company from the U.K. and Steve Munch, Mandy Frost and Don Harvey watched it on a monitor in their conference room.

I know what was said behind my back that day because recently Don Harvey told me about it and gave me a transcript of the tape. He turned out to be a pretty good guy after all was said and done. Very helpful. Here's the transcript. The reporter was a beautiful brunette "talking head" named Laura Lance.

LAURA: Uncle John, the self-styled zombie, has become a tabloid sensation, here as well as in America. Whether or not he is who he says he is -- or the kind of *creature* he says he is -- millions of people are utterly fascinated. Rumor is that he has gotten a six-figure advance for a new book entitled *My Life as a Zombie*, to be co-written by him and John Russo who actually played a zombie in *Night of the Living Dead*. We're proud to bring you this exclusive interview with Uncle John's niece. Cy-Fi, do tell us what your day-to-day life is like with your uncle.

CY-FI: I know your viewers want to hear something bizarre or sensational, Laura, but the truth is that our lives are mostly pretty mundane. As I've said, Uncle John is just a regular guy with unusual dietary considerations. There are lots of things he wishes he could still do, but

he's had to adapt. He still likes to read a lot, though.

LAURA: He still keeps up with what's going on in the world?

CY-FI: Oh, yes, definitely! Your listeners will learn that if they will log in to his podcast. He's a liberal Democrat. He voted in our last mid-term election. I took him to the polling place. One of the volunteers gave us some flack, she didn't like the way he looked, but we shut her up when we produced his voter ID.

LAURA: I understand voter repression is a big problem in your country.

CY-FI: Mostly it's directed against poor people and minorities, but it can be that much more difficult if you happen to be a zombie.

LAURA: I can imagine. But on the other hand your notoriety has helped you in some ways, hasn't it? I understand that you and Uncle John now have a nightclub act. A noted critic has called you "the supernatural Sonny and Cher."

CY-FI: Well, we're just two ordinary people trying to get along in the world in spite of the hand that's been dealt to us. That's been our main point all along.

LAURA: I assure you that the British people are pulling for you, Cy-Fi. Thanks for this exclusive interview.

CY-FI: My pleasure.

LAURA: This is Laura Lance signing off from the United Kingdom.

Steve Munch picked up a Remote and hit Rewind. "My God," he said. "We've created a monster!"

Mandy said, "He already *was* a monster."

Munch said, "But we've made it worse. Look at the exposure he's getting. I wouldn't be

surprised to see him land a Hollywood agent."

"He's probably already got one," Laura said, enviously.

Don Harvey grimaced at the thought. "I hope not," he said. "Not till we've gotten all we can out of him. And his niece and nephew."

Munch said, "Well, all three of them will be at the press conference we're covering tonight. That should give us some good stuff, boss."

"I hope so," Don Harvey said. "I don't want to see our ratings in the shitter again."

The press conference they were talking about was at a Marriott in a room lit up with so much bright fluorescence that it showed all my facial defects. No dark, shadowy places to soften my image. I didn't feel so good about myself when I popped into a men's room and looked at myself in a mirror destroying the illusion that I looked pretty good in my bright red Wrangler shirt and black Wrangler trousers. Oscar was wearing his security guard uniform, as usual, and was lurking around watching out for trouble. Cy-Fi wore a great-looking black gown with a lacy low-cut bodice. She and I sat behind a long desk with a couple of microphones. Everybody else sat in folding chairs facing us. The room was full. Lots of reporters and lots of zombies, both real and fake. But the ones in makeup were so realistic, for the most part, that I had trouble telling them apart from the genuine article. So I just played everything straight. I didn't challenge anyone and neither did Cy-Fi. We had discussed this beforehand and had decided to just take them all at their word. A shudder went through me when I pictured ICE showing up like the Gestapo and herding us away in chains -- even though I knew that the Supreme Court had temporarily blocked the President's Executive Order.

Cy-Fi opened up the proceedings: "I'm glad to see so many of you at our press conference, especially our civic-minded ZPS members."

I backed her up, saying, "Yes, indeed. Thanks to our Zombie Protection Society, someday I may be able to sit on our front porch without fear of a drive-by."

"We're hoping to make the world safe for zombies," Cy-Fi said proudly. Mandy Frost and Steve Munch are here from FLSH-TV giving us valuable coverage. We deeply appreciate their efforts."

In the back of the room, with a big camera on a tripod, Many and Munch waved at the audience. I supposed that with the brightness of the room they needed only the camera, no hot movie lights.

"Will it be on the six o'clock news?" someone called out. But I didn't see who. I mean was it a reporter or a zombie?

"We don't know when it will run yet," Cy-Fi said. "Save that question for later and maybe Mandy will clue us in."

My voice was froggy today, and I apologized. "Sorry for the way I sound. I have a little rigor mortis in my vocal chords. It goes away mostly, when I exercise and when Cy-Fi gives me a special blend of her own invention. I think she spikes it with Viagra."

This got some amused titters from the crowd and a good-looking female reporter piped up, a bit embarrassed. "You mean you can get..." She succumbed to shyness and didn't finish the implication.

"Certainly," I told her, and she giggled and looked away.

I refrained from explaining that Dr. Delbert Strange was correct when he determined that the part of the nervous system that affects erectile function is separate from the part that controls other basic functions. I don't know why sex is so embarrassing to Americans, whereas in most European countries they have it in a much healthier perspective. Repressed sexual urges lead to perversion. I think that some people who are ashamed and extremely guilty of their homosexual leanings (or even their heterosexual desires) will enter the priesthood in hopes that becoming "holy" and purportedly "sacrificing sex for God" will help them control those leanings. But the need for sex cannot be totally and determinedly thwarted. Celibacy is de facto abnormal. The urges that one tries to tamp down will sometimes come bursting out in a perverse form such as the sexual abuse of women or even children.

Cy-Fy said, "Uncle John doesn't have a girlfriend these days because women are afraid of him. But they don't need to be. He would never force himself on anyone. He's not that way. No matter how famous he may get, he will never use his fame to gain power over anybody. He will never be accused of groping or making unwanted sexual advances like so many of our movie stars and top politicians have been doing."

While I was listening to Cy-Fi and appreciating her nice comments about me, I saw Mandy Frost working her way toward Oscar, then sidling up to him and putting a hand on his big barrel-like chest. What the hell was that all about? It looked like she might be trying to seduce him. He was shy and clumsy with women, and he had never had a girlfriend and badly desired one. So he was terribly susceptible to the charms of any woman who wanted to manipulate him.

Cy-Fi told the crowd, "Uncle John and I are going to talk a bit about what our daily life is like, then we're going to do our Q&A."

We had discussed the format of the press conference beforehand, and she was adhering to it. During this part of it, we covered much of the ground we had already covered on television and in my blogs and podcasts, knowing that most of the reporters present would not have had time to watch and listen in detail until now. We purposely made our daily lives sound tame and mundane because we were out to convince everybody that zombies don't really need to be feared *all* the time, but only when we're hungry. At other times, people like me have a lot to contribute to society.

Just then, to my chagrin, I saw Detective Jane Smart come into the room and glare at me in contempt and disbelief. Obviously she didn't think I was apt to contribute anything of value. I was sure that she desired nothing more than to end my contributions permanently. Yet, unless I was fooling myself, I thought that the sneer on her face weakened a little when Cy-Fi and I began elaborating upon our political beliefs. I dared to hope that perhaps Jane, unlike most cops, was a liberal, like me maybe we had struck some empathy in her heart when we revealed that we were avid contributors, not just to the Zombie Protection Society but also to the ACLU, the Family Planning Council, Black Lives Matter and even Blue Lives Matter.

Our goal was to soften the public attitude toward us. We wanted people to understand that we had common ground with everybody, not just zombies. We wanted to help our country step back, take an introspective look at itself and aspire once more to what George H.W. Bush had termed "a kinder and gentler America."

But when we segued into the Q&A nobody wanted to talk about politics or social issues.

They were doggedly focused on the uniqueness of my "life after death" and my dramatic appearance on the public landscape.

The fellow who earlier had asked the question about the six o'clock news rose to his feet and I now could see what I hadn't been sure of before: he was a zombie. He had a brush cut and was stylishly dressed in a white shirt and black slacks, but his face was scarred, partly decayed and greenish looking. In a raspy voice he said, "My name is Marvin. I'm a zombie just like you, Uncle John, and I've had to spend the last ten years in hiding. I'd like to thank you and your niece for giving me some hope that after all this time I may be able to finally come out of the closet."

"Are you gay?" one of the reporters stupidly blurted.

"No! Absolutely not!" Marvin shouted indignantly. "Gays have it hard enough, but they're accepted these days and can even get married. What about *us*, though? People don't want to recognize that we're just as human as *they* are!"

"I don't blame you for being upset," Cy-Fi said.

A portly middle-aged woman sitting next to Marvin stood up and patted his head. "I'm his mom," she said. "There are mothers all across the United States who are hiding their sons and daughters in attics and basements. Yet we have the nerve to call ourselves the Greatest Nation on Earth -- which when you think about it insults all the other countries. Marvin and I have both joined the Zombie Protection Society, and we urge all of you to do the same! We have to break the political gridlock that stops real progress from being made in this country!"

She got a smattering of applause from about half of our audience, and I was grateful for it. I even thought I saw Jane Smart nod her head involuntarily. The fact that the entire audience didn't applaud showed how far we still had to go. Half the people in the United States still vote against their own best interests and the President is a master of getting them to do so.

Another zombie piped up with a question. He might have been a real zombie, I couldn't decide. He was one of those whose makeup -- if it *was* makeup -- was pretty convincing. He said, "How's come if you can think and talk, something can't be done about your face? You don't look too good, if you don't mind my saying so."

So once again we were back to straight zombie questions and off of politics and social issues. But it couldn't be helped. So I answered politely.

"Dr. Strange told me that the ugly color in my face is lividity," I explained. "When you're dead your blood sinks to the lowest part of your body and turns purple, like a bruise. I must've been lying flat on my face at some point, for a long time. For all I know, I might have slipped on a banana peel and fell down really hard -- like that girl's snotty brother, Johnny, who got his head smashed against a tombstone."

"Seems like I've seen that movie before," he said with a chuckle.

A gray-haired female reporter with a press badge that said NEW YORK TIMES raised her hand and asked, "How do you relate to other zombies? Do you fight over what you're going to eat?"

"Not usually," I said. "Zombies are willing to share, they have manners just like regular people. But now and then there are those who want to hog all the good parts, the delicacies. We have good conversation while we're eating. Some funny stuff happens sometimes, though. One day a bunch of us were having a snack -- if you know what I mean -- and telling tales about how we had died. And one fellow's pants were down around his ankles and he was hobbling around, trying to figure out how to get them the rest of the way off, past his shoes. I could see his junk was gone, I mean he didn't have anything down there, he was like Barbie's boyfriend Ken, only a lot bloodier and messier in his pubic area, it wasn't a clean surgical removal. He told us he got drunk on a golf course and he bet his buddy twenty bucks he could wash his balls in the ball-washing machine -- and he didn't mean his golf balls!"

I laughed just telling that story, and so did the audience. I was learning that I could be damned entertaining when I wanted to be.

While I was into all that, Mandy actually was coming on to Oscar, but at the time I didn't know the full extent of her wily ways. Oscar eventually told me about the whole deal, not only what happened that day but afterwards, and that's why I can accurately report what went on between them. Smiling a fake smile, Mandy reached out and plucked some imaginary lint from his security guard shirt -- and he backed away from her a little bit, flustered but also flattered.

"Don't be scared of me, I like you," Mandy whispered.

"You're not gonna worm anything outta me," Oscar said staunchly. "Cy-Fi told me to watch out for you."

"Doesn't she want you to get any attention?" Mandy purred. "She must want it all for herself."

"She's just smarter'n me, and I guess I know it."

"So you let her boss you around! Does she ever let you go out on a date?"

Embarrassed, he said nothing, and Mandy got bolder.

"Would it freak her out if she knew you had sex with me?"

Oscar turned beet red, and Mandy pressed her advantage. "Are you still a virgin, Oscar? If so, I'd like very much to help you change that."

Meanwhile, Cy-Fi and I were wrapping up the press conference. She said to the crowd, "It was so much fun being here! I hope you all learned something!"

While all this was going on between Oscar and Mandy (which, as I said, I didn't find out about till much later), I told another true story to the press conference attendees. I wanted to give them plenty to write about so we'd get big coverage and great publicity for my podcast. My third story was about a woman who had an abusive husband, and I hoped that what had happened to him would not only shed light but help put a damper on that sort of behavior.

"This young girl's husband was beating her up all the time and she got so she couldn't take it anymore, so she hanged herself in their bathroom. He came home from a drinking binge, went in there to take a leak and found her there, still twitching. He got a knife from drawer in the kitchen and cut her down, figuring he might save her and keep on making a punching bag out of her from then on. But the joke was on him. She wasn't dead she was *un*dead! And as soon as he untied the noose, she jumped at him and bit into his neck! Both of them were later shot by the cops."

This got a lot of *oohs* and *aws* from the audience. And I hoped they would take this very serious matter to heart. The lady from the *New York Times* was the only one who made a comment, though. She said she was pleasantly surprised that I was so deeply concerned about social issues even though I was who I was.

After the press conference broke up, I had to urgently go to the men's room -- and Jane Smart barged right in on me. She didn't have her gun drawn, but she startled me nonetheless.

Ever since I became like this, my urine has had a greenish tinge to it, and she grimaced when she saw that. "You claim you're a zombie, but you still have to pee?" she said disdainfully. "And it's such a creepy color."

I said, "I'm pretty normal in most ways, babe -- including the ones that count."

Picking up on my innuendo, she said, "They don't count with me. Zip up. Get your hands behind your back, buster."

"Let me shake the drips first. Unless *you* want to."

"Okay, Mr. Wise Guy. Let's go!"

She ushered me out and we bumped into Cy-Fi, who was immediately alarmed. "Where are you taking him?" she demanded.

"Down to the station. I have questions to ask him and I don't want you around. Wait here. I'll bring him back when I'm finished with him."

"You'd better -- if you don't want sued for wrongful arrest."

"Hah! I don't think you'll get anywhere with that," Jane said.

When we got to the police station, she put me in an interrogation room, under a bright light. It wasn't a *hot* light, but it was the only light in the room, shining down on both of us, so that the rest of the room was shrouded in partial darkness. Right away I showed her that I knew my rights, even though my hands were cuffed in back of the chair rungs. I said, "I'm not as brain dead as you think I am. I have a right to remain silent, I have a right to an attorney, and I have a right to make a phone call, and I want to talk with my niece. Right now!"

She said, "You're not under arrest yet, so I don't have to read you your rights."

"Then why am I in handcuffs?"

"As a precaution. You're delusional. You think you're a zombie. So you might try to bite me. And for all I know you might have an STD."

"I wish. It'd almost be worth getting the clap if I could get some nookie once in a while."

"You're claiming you still get horny?"

"I get so horny you wouldn't believe. But there aren't too many babes who want to have sex with a zombie. I've been hoping to find a cute little necrophiliac, but so far no luck. Let's go to bed. You can keep the handcuffs on me."

She backed away and shot me a hateful look. Then she said, "Look here, Uncle John. If you're a real zombie, as you claim, I could shoot you in the head right now and it'd be perfectly legal. All I'd have to do is write up a report and haul your ass to a crematorium."

Well, I couldn't take that kind of disrespect, even from her, and even though I was so attracted to her. "My niece would sue you in civil court," I threatened. "You can't just go around

shooting innocent people."

"You mutilated a corpse. Then you ate part of him."

"You might think that, but you can't prove it."

"Oscar carries a gun. I can get a warrant and have it test-fired. If it matches the slugs taken out of Clyde Yancey, Oscar will be sent up and he'll do hard time. That I can guarantee."

"My nephew doesn't have that gun anymore. He lost it. He had a different one just like it. So there."

"You won't stymie me much longer. I'm on to you, and I'm not going to stop till I put you away."

Just to jerk her around (and maybe with a little bit of hopefulness) I said, "You know, we might be temporary enemies, but I think you're cute. I'd really like to take you to bed. Why don't you give me a break?"

"No way!" she snapped. "Shut up, or I really will shoot you! Right now!"

"C'mon, babe. Loosen up. We can do it doggy style. You won't even have to look at me."

She got up, stomped out of the interrogation room and left me there for a long time, in handcuffs, till finally the desk sergeant came and unlocked them. If you've never been suffering from rigor mortis and in handcuffs, I assure you that you don't want to try it.

I made it out to the curb and was massaging my wrists and waiting for Cy-Fi to pull up to the curb in the 1967 Le Mans when a TV reporter sneaked around the corner of the yellow brick building and started bugging me for an interview. He wasn't from FLSH-TV, it was some other station. I finally gave in and said, "I'll answer a few questions, but you better hurry up because

as soon as my niece shows up I'm gone."

He started speaking a mile a minute into his microphone even as his cameraman hustled toward us with his camera on a shoulder pod.

"This is Cameron Quinn on the air with the so-called Zombie Sensation who has millions of people intrigued and excited. So, Uncle John, can we talk about diet?"

"Everybody wants to talk about that! I keep telling them I'm not much different from a person with food allergies. I can't eat a lot of things -- I have to discipline myself. I need to get regular feedings of one particular kind of food. But I don't like to make a big deal out of what kind it happens to be."

Cameron Quinn backed off a little, saying, "All right, I can respect that. I realize it's a touchy subject, so let's move on."

"I'm ready and willing to do just that," I told him. "Because I've had a rough day and I need a pick-me-up. I'd like to chomp into *you*. Your chubby cheeks look pretty darn tasty."

When he heard that, he backed away from me a few more feet and started really hurrying up his questions. "Your niece is a fire breather, so I wonder if she cooks for you. Does she *seer* your food items for you, so they're easier to chew and digest? And does she use any special seasoning?   And what's it like to digest human meat?"

"I refuse to answer on the grounds that it may incriminate me."

With a beaming smile, he spoke gleefully into the camera. "You just witnessed a *first*, folks! Right here on the Cameron Quinn Show, an actual walking, talking *zombie* has pleaded the Fifth Amendment!"

The next morning I was mentioned for the first time in a tweet from the President of the United States:

"Uncle John must be put down whether he's a zombie or not. He's a mockery to the court system I've been loading with wonderful amazing people. Zombies have no rights! Liberals think they do. Sad! #WH."

CHAPTER 14

Zombies on the Loose

Stush was sitting at a card table in his rustic hunting lodge of hand-hewn logs, with a cash box in front of him. Resting on the dark-stained mantle of a huge stone fireplace was a flat-screen TV that was always tuned to Faux News, Stush's favorite station. His political views were decidedly right-wing, constantly aided and abetted by a raft of blond talking heads who could all have been named Heathers and slickly dressed men with razor-cut hair spray-canned in place, who seemed to work themselves into fits of anger directed against liberals before they went on the air.

On the TV, a panel of broadcasters was heaping praise upon the Tweeter-in-Chief. Stush, who used to be a teenaged skinhead ad used to love beating up gays, was glad to see the Faux News personalities lauding the Administration's stance against letting transsexuals continue to serve in the military.

Dan, Joe and Judy barged into the lodge, heavily armed, and Joe stepped up to the card table and plunked down a thick wad of money, saying, "Here's my two grand, Stush. I don't know what kinda special thing you got planned for us today, but I sure hope it's worth my time."

"It will be," Stush said. "We're gonna turn a pack of our zombies loose in the woods and you hunt 'em down and shoot 'em. But if you screw up there's a pretty good chance they might turn the tables on you."

Judy said, "You mean we might get chomped on?"

"That's it," said Stush. "But that's the chance you agreed to take. It'll make things more exciting. If you want out, tell me right now and I'll refund your deposit."

"I'm *in*," Judy said. "I'm in, Stush, don't try to talk me out of it!"

"Ain't no zombie gonna sneak up on me," Dan boasted. I'm a skilled woodsman -- and an expert tracker. I poached lions and tigers in Africa and made a bundle offa their skins and never got bit. I blasted down elephants and rhinos too, and the natives ground their horns up and made aphrodisiacs. They work pretty good. Wanna try some, Judy?"

She sneered at him and said, "My bar ain't that low." Which was her usual comeback.

Joe said, "Zombies are a piece of cake 'cause they're fucked up in the head. Lions and tigers are a lot bigger challenge. They got their wits about them, and zombies don't."

"Hey, Stush," Judy said, "if you're gonna turn them loose in the woods, they could just wander off, couldn't they? What's to stop them?"

Stush said, "For one thing, they can't run. They don't have enough strength or coordination."

"But I'm paying you good money," said Judy, "and I wanna know what's to stop your zombies from getting loose and maybe gobbling up a kid or two and bringing the heat down on us. Don't you remember what happened to that pro quarterback just for lynching a couple of pit bulls?"

Up to the challenge, Stush grinned and said, ""Well, for another thing, Miss Smartypants, Sam and Hal are herding them out of the cage one at a time and fastening monitors on them like the things dogs wear instead of chains, when their owners wanna keep 'em from leavin' the yard but don't wanna chain 'em up. Our zombies can't really wander farther than a slice of the woods that we ringed with those little sonic ray kinda thingies that give 'em a shock if they violate the boundaries."

"A *shock!*" Dan said. "How do we know a fuckin' zombie can even *feel* that?"

"Because we tested 'em!" Stush barked. "You're exasperatin' me with all these stupid fuckin' questions. If you don't wanna kill zombies, why don't you all go home and tend to your knitting or crocheting or crossword puzzles or whatever? Make up your minds -- do you belong here or not?"

"I do!" Joe said. "I like it, Stush. You're sayin' we can have a field day flushin' 'em out, huntin' 'em down and shootin' 'em in the head!"

"Well, you gotta watch out for 'em, though. They can also have a field day chompin' on *you* if you let 'em get the jump on ya."

***

In preparation for the upcoming hunt, six zombies had been driven out of the cage by Sam and Hal, using cattle prods. They poked at the zombies, continually zapping them -- with loud sizzles and sparks -- in order to start driving them up a hill and into the woods to be hunted down just for fun. Before doing that, they counted the zombies still left, and there were eight of them that were not needed for the hunt, and one of them was Betty Montgomery, the young woman who had been kidnapped, tied to a stake, then bitten by a zombie so that she would turn into one.

"Her body ain't rotted too much," Sam said. "She still looks sorta good in that teeny yellow bikini."

Hal said, "Careful, Sam! We gotta keep the sparks from the cattle prods to a bare minimum! They're just dead flesh -- they go up pretty easy!"

"Now, where've I heard that before?" Sam said.

They both snickered because Hal's last sentence was an iconic line spoken by Sheriff McClellan in *Night of the Living Dead*, a movie they had both watched about a hundred times.

Hal said, "Be careful, we don't want 'em to go up in flames, like those crazy monks in

Tibet who used to commit' suicide by settin' themselves on fire."

They kept prodding the zombies and yelling at them to keep moving, just as if they were trying to wrangle spooked cattle. But the zombies were growling and hissing and trying to turn around and bite them.

Sam yelled, "*Shoo, goddamn it!* I know you're slow-movin' but right now you're just bein' *lazy!*"

Hal said, "Maybe they can sense what's gonna happen to 'em -- like cows penned up in the slaughter house."

"I don't think they sense a damn thing," Sam said. "Hey, wait a minute! Where's that female one -- Betty?"

"I thought we was s'posed to leave her behind. Stush said we c'd use her to create more zombies."

"He changed his mind, says he wants a female for 'em to hunt this time, for variety. They been lobbyin' him for it, gettin' on his nerves."

"Let's go get her then."

They pushed and prodded some more, till they got the six zombies scared and agitated enough to keep on heading up the hill on their own. Then they turned around and headed back to the cage. Through the steel mesh, they eyed the one named Betty, who along with the others was staring at Sam and Hal and drooling at the thought of their tasty flesh. The hideous, rasping sound made by the zombies built to a fever pitch.

Hal said, "Push the prod through the links over there, Sam. Get her stunned and afraid of us, then we'll open the cage and get her out."

Sam moved in close, poked his prod through the steel links of the cage and right into Betty's chest. He zapped her three times in rapid succession. She moved back, making a high-pitched warbling growl that was almost feminine. Then Hal opened the cage, keeping his eyes warily on Betty at all times.

Hal said, "Quick! Hand me somethin' from the cooler!"

"Comin' up!" Sam answered.

He stooped, opened a Coleman chest that held a couple of body parts on ice. He pulled out a naked detached foot and handed it to

Hal, who said, "I don't trust her one bit. She's a mean little bitch, droolin' her ass off like she ain't never had nothin' to eat."

Sam speculated, "Maybe the older and bigger ones push her away from the food. She mighta never got to bite into Reverend Hotchkiss—even though we cut him up into little pieces.

She'll get to taste him now, though. I handed you one of the leftovers."

Hal said, "When I lure her out, lasso her, Sam!"

He picked up a lariat hanging on a nail in a nearby tree. Meanwhile, Sam held out the severed foot toward Betty, and she started to come after it. But Sam kept backing away, making her pursue the "food" so she had to come out of the cage. Then Hal dropped his lasso around Betty's neck.

But -- surprise!-- Betty seized the rest of the rope in her two hands, getting Hal off balance and quickly pulling him toward her -- then chomping into his throat!

Reacting quickly, even though he was scared out of his wits, Sam tried to save Hal by yanking his revolver out and blasting Betty in the head. She reeled back against the steel cage, then fell to the concrete floor, a bloody chunk of Hal's neck still clenched in her ghoulish teeth.

Sam slammed the door of the cage shut, hurriedly locked it, and ran into the hunting lodge where Stush was sitting behind his card table and having an argument with Judy.

"I watchin' my TV in peace till you started raggin' on me!" he told her indignantly. He hated for anyone to interrupt him when he was glued to Faux News.

"You shorted me!" she accused him. "I had five kills, not four!"

Sam yelled, "Bad news, boss! That Betty zombie turned on Hal in the cage and bit him! Now he's gonna turn into one of 'em!"

Stush said, "Well, the hunters can shoot him on the next hunt. Just clean the mess up and hose out the cage."

Sam yanked out his revolver and yelled in Stush's face. "You rotten motherfucker! My brother is gonna turn into a zombie and all you can say is clean out the mess? I oughta drill you right now, you no-good bastard!"

He pushed the barrel of his gun right up against Stush's forehead and Stush jumped back, looking scared. But before Sam could pull the trigger -- *Blam!!* Judy shot him in the back, and he dropped at her feet. But he was writhing around, groaning, not dead yet, so she finished him off by putting a bullet in his head.

"Good move, Judy!" Stush said. "Now he's zombie feed."

"Show your appreciation by straightening out my pay," Judy said. "Have it ready when I get back. I've gotta join Dan and Joe up on the hill."

***

Within the next half hour, the three hunters -- Dan, Joe and Judy -- were making their way through the woods, their eyes peeled for lurking zombies. They were keyed up, seeking to spot a tell-tale footprint or a shred of partially decayed skin hanging from a branch -- or for hearing the crunch of dead leaves or the crack of a twig.

Joe Talerico thought he'd do better on his own, so he said, "I'm gonna head down the other way. If I spot any of 'em I won't hog the shots. I'll give ya a yell."

"Liar!" Judy said.

Joe snickered and went his own way.

Dan said to Judy, "I don't think they'll try to make it through dense underbrush, it's too hard for them. They'll either try to hide, or if they're on the move they'll stick to the paths."

She shot back, "I already thought of that. I don't need your help or your dumb opinions, Dan. Just because I'm a woman, you think you're superior to me."

"I'm just making conversation. Why don't you give me a break, Judy?"

"Why? So you can get in my pants?"

"I'd be the best lay you ever had. But if you wanna deprive yourself -- *AaaagghhHHH!*"

He cried out because -- just at that moment -- a zombie lying in a ditch, right at his feet, grabbed him by his ankles and pulled him down. Going down, he tried to maintain a grip on his rifle, but failed. Two more zombies pounced on him, and he clawed for a grip on his rifle but it was out of reach.

Judy was stunned. She ran back a piece and thought she would just keep on running, leaving Dan to his fate. But then she decided to do the right thing, not out of a sense of decency, but out of knowing that the other hunters would dump on her if they found she had chickened out.

By this time the three zombies were biting Dan all over, on every exposed part of his body -- wrists, calves, face and neck.

Judy aimed from about twenty feet away and blasted one of the zombies in the head with her rifle. The impact knocked him backwards and he fell dead.

A second zombie was hungrily ripping at Dan when Judy fired again and killed him.

She stepped closer to the third zombie to make sure of her shot -- but then the zombie grabbed hold of the barrel and they got into a tug-of-war for her weapon.

Judy managed to point the rifle at the zombie, but at his chest, not his head. She squeezed the trigger anyway -- but the bullet passed harmlessly through the zombie's body, plowing a path through rotted, flying flesh. He fell down, but started to get up. Greenish blood leaked out between his fingers. A sickening look on his face, he got to his feet, but Judy blasted him in his head and he was done for.

With zombie bodies lying all around, she looked down at Dan, who was slumped against a tree, bleeding from multiple zombie bites.

Joe Talerico came running up, from out of the woods somewhere. "Damn it!" he said. "I had a bead on one of 'em but the racket from over here made me jerk my trigger finger and the shot went wide!"

Judy said, pointing with her rifle barrel, "That zombie right there got the jump on Dan and all hell broke loose. They almost got *me!*"

"Well, it sounded like the Fourth of July over here. What're we gonna do about Dan?"

Dan piped up, obviously weak and fading fast. "Just do what you gotta do."

"We can drag you back down to the lodge, maybe. If you can last."

"No! I don't wanna turn into of *them!* Shoot me in the head."

Joe said, "That'd be murder -- 'cause you ain't turned yet."

"I don't care," Dan said, his voice hoarse and getting weaker. "Nobody will find out you shot me up here, long as you two keep mum about it."

Joe said, "You look like you ain't gonna last long, Dan. Why don't we wait till you turn, *then* shoot ya?"

But Dan was wary of this. He said, "I know you, Joe. You might wanna give me chance to get away, then come after me."

Judy said, "He's got a point, Joe. After he turns, if he retains a bit of intelligence for a while, he might be a challenge to bring down."

Mulling it over, Joe said, "We better bring him back and let Stush make the decision."

But Dan pleaded, "Just *shoot* me, for God's sake!"

"Now, don't get all antsy, Dan, we wanna deliberate and make sure we do the right thing."

Growing weak yet, Dan said, "The...right...thing is...to do away with me...right now. Have a heart...I can't..."

Too weak to talk any longer, he managed a few ragged last breaths, then coughed blood and died as Joe and Judy looked on.

Smirking, Judy said, "I gotta confess I never really liked him very much. He was a know-it-all, always actin' like he was too good for the rest of us. I think we've got a right to let him turn into one of *them* -- and then have some fun huntin' him down."

Liking the idea, Joe said, "We could do it up right, babe. Get away from him a ways and let him turn, then give him a good head start.

You and I separate in the meantime, then we have us a little contest. I bet five bucks I get him before you do."

"Don't be a piker. Let's make it a hundred bucks," Judy said.

"Deal!" Joe said.

Grinning at each other, they shook hands, bumped fists, and put the plan into action.

CHAPTER 15

Jane Interrogates Mandy

Mandy Frost was in a chair getting makeup touched up by FLSH-TV cosmetic expert, when Jane Smart barged in on her. Mandy was annoyed, even though she had consented to the appointment. She said, "All right, Detective Smart, you asked for this meeting. I'm on the air in five minutes, so let's get it over with."

"I expect your full cooperation, Mandy. I'm trying to solve a murder."

"Clyde Yancey? Don't tell me you suspect Uncle John. He's not strong enough and probably not even smart enough."

(I hope Mandy didn't actually mean that. I choose to believe that she was disparaging me on purpose because she didn't want me to get arrested. I was good for selling sponsorships, and she had other plans for me that went beyond her interest in keeping me as a ratings booster. But right then, of course, I had no idea what those other plans were.)

Jane said, "I don't think he did the actual shooting. Or the butchering."

"You must have your eye on his niece and nephew."

"Of course I do. They probably did the dirty deed, but he got the benefits. Under the law, he's as guilty as they are and I want to see that they're all punished."

"So what do I have to do with that?"

"You've been hanging out with them, interviewing them, putting them on the air. You know more about them than anyone else does. So give me your honest opinion. Do you think it's possible that they shot Clyde Yancey and fed part of him to their uncle?"

"Sure, it's possible. But if I knew as much as you think I know, my audience would hear it first."

Jane said sharply, "If you're withholding evidence in a murder case, it makes you guilty of conspiracy. Or aiding and abetting. Or both."

Unfazed, Mandy said, "Listen Detective Smart, I don't have any evidence to withhold, and you don't have any evidence against *me*. So this conversation is over."

"If I find out you're lying to me," Jane threatened, "you'll be prosecuted to the fullest extent of the law."

"Haw! You have no grounds for your suspicions, you're just fishing. And by the way, if I had known what they were up to, I'd have wanted to film it. What an exclusive!"

"Yes indeed, Mandy! The kind of exclusive that could put you away for a long, long time. Do you swing both ways? Because you will, once those horny prisoners get hold of a beautiful talking head like you."

"Well, that'd be an exclusive, too," said Mandy.

After she taped her show that day, which for once had nothing to do with Uncle John,

she consented to speak with Sheriff McClelland, who had come in without an appointment. He was still big news these days due to the fact that he had been accused of shooting a black man fifty years ago and labeling it a case of mistaken identity. He was a grizzled old man now, and she thought she could just intimidate him and get the meeting over with.

She sat him down in the conference room and said perfunctorily, "Listen, Sheriff, we here at FLSH-TV are well aware that you're under fire for the way you conducted yourself during the first zombie epidemic decades ago. But many people nowadays have a much more enlightened attitude toward zombies than the general public used to have back then."

He said, "You got that right, Mandy. All we knew then was they were dangerous and we had to kill 'em -- so that's what we did. Nobody was talkin' about rehab or cures or nothin' like that. This

Uncle John character has stirred up a lot of shit and it's all comin' down on *me*."

"It's not his fault, Sheriff. He's got his own agenda. You're just collateral damage."

"Everybody was mighty grateful once upon a time when they were scared shitless -- but now it's a different story. I just want you to put me on the air so I can tell my side of it."

Mandy said, "I don't blame you for being bitter, but you must admit that black man didn't deserve to die. It was a major blunder on your part, wouldn't you say so?"

"That's easy to say for folks that never saw that kinda combat. They're nothin' but lousy chicken hawks, the kind that swift-boated John Kerry and wanna impeach our damned fine President. If it wasn't for Black Lives Matter and all the other nuts that go around bitching about everything, I'd be home free."

"I'm afraid your true colors are coming out, Sheriff, and I'm appalled! You keep spouting off like that, you're sure to get convicted. You'd better watch your mouth!"

"You're just like the rest of 'em. You won't give me a chance."

"Even if I agreed with you on your hard-right attitudes, I still couldn't put you on the air right now. Uncle John is big news. He's our bread and butter during ratings season. And if we would pit you up against him we'd be cutting off our nose to spite our face."

"You mean you're not gonna let me speak my piece?"

"I'm sorry, but we can't do it right now. It's too risky. Come back six months from now. When Uncle John is old news."

"Damn it, Mandy, by that time I'll be hung out to dry!" the sheriff barked. And then he stormed out of the conference room.

He was so angry and depressed that he jumped into his beat-up Volkswagen and headed straight to Stush Polanski's hunting camp. You see, all the while that he was protesting his innocence in the matter of Ben's death, he had been coming to the camp and paying money out of his meager Social Security check for the privilege of killing zombies. He was an out-and-out hypocrite.

He was so enfeebled by old age, arthritis and other maladies that he was unable to tromp through the woods and up and down hills like the other hunters did, so Stush would set him up at a firing table outside the lodge and turn a few "easy kill" zombies loose in the nearby field.

A young black girl was already at the firing station that day, getting her first taste of the experience. Her name was Ophelia, and she was already fuming about seeing the sheriff on TV and having to endure his claims of innocence. Before he even got there, she was bitching at Joe and Judy. "Did you hear about that nasty old sheriff getting indicted? It's about time! I hope he gets what he deserves! It's been a long time comin'!"

Judy said, "Get off it, Ophelia. I don't think he was a racist, he was just doing his job."

"What're you? A redneck apologist? He killed Ben, and he done it on purpose, that's a fuckin' fact, sure as I'm standin' here! If he was in front of me right now I'd put one between his eyes!"

Joe said, "Oh, come on, girl, why don't you let bygones be bygones?"

"Because black folks are still getting killed by the cops! I warn you, don't none of you shoot at those white ones in the field -- they're for me! I'll teach that damn sheriff! If he can shoot only black ones, I'm only gonna shoot *white* ones! I hope they hang his ass!"

At that moment Sheriff McClelland came out of the lodge carrying his deer hunting rifle, and he had a sheepish look on his face because he had overheard Ophelia's rant.

"I got *your* number!" she blurted. "You're in big trouble finally, for shooting Ben! How's come there was more white zombies than black ones back then, yet you shot only black ones?"

"Bullshit! I shot all kinds of 'em! Even Chinese ones!"

"I oughta drill you right now!" Ophelia said. And she pulled a revolver on him.

Stush heard them arguing and came out of the lodge, drawing his own pistol. "Shut the fuck up!" he shouted. "*Both* of you! You're gettin' on my fuckin' nerves!"

"I'll shut *him* up!" Ophelia yelled back at Stush.

She shot the sheriff in the head, and his brains splattered against the stone wall of the lodge.

Without a second of hesitation, Stush shot Ophelia in her chest and she slumped over the firing table with a gaping exit hole in her back.

"Zombie feed!" Stush said. "Anybody who gives me any shit gets turned into zombie feed!" He tucked his gun in his belt and went back into the lodge.

Later that same day, there was yet another unfortunate incident. Three hunters who were new at the game had paid big bucks for a night shooting. And one of them, named Chris, had lost his legs in a house fire and was in a wheelchair. His two buddies, rough-looking guys in black outfits like those worn by Navy Seals, were named Landon and Brad.

Stush had arranged for another pack of zombies to be turned loose in the field, and there was a bright enough moon for the shooters to take a good aim at their targets. Soon as they saw zombies staggering around at there, they started blasting away with rifles and shotguns. All the zombies went down, and Brad said, "I'm goin' out there and check my kills."

Landon finished off a can of Iron City beer and said, "I got everything I aimed at, and I'm damn sure of it. I'm gonna stick around here and drink some more."

"Wheel me out there," Chris said. "I wanna check my kills, too. I got the one who was munchin' on a piece of somebody's leg."

Brad wheeled Chris out to where six of the zombies lay still, spread out in almost a semi-circle on the grass. The one who had been munching on part of a human leg now lay still, flat on her face, with the leg sticking out from under her.

But she wasn't dead yet -- and suddenly she rolled over, grabbed Brad by the ankle and bit into his calf.

Brad fell down, and Chris, in trying to get away, tumbled out of his wheelchair.

Landon had just come out of the lodge with another can of Iron City, and when he saw what was happening, he shot the female zombie who had bitten Brad right in her forehead. She went down heavily, with not just the hole in her head bloody, but also her mouth and lips -- from Brad's blood.

Chris stopped crawling and sat up and looked closely at Brad, just as Landon got there.

"You wanna shoot him, or should I do it?" Landon asked.

"He's our *buddy* for chrissake!" Chris pouted. And he started to cry.

"Man up!" Landon ordered. "Shooting him is the right thing to do, and both of us know it."

"I'll do it," Chris said, wiping his tears with a red bandana. "It's my fault. I asked him to wheel me out here."

"It was his idea, too," Landon reminded. "But it'll do you good to work up the nerve to do it."

"I know it has to be done," Brad said. "Go ahead, Chris. You have my blessing."

"We'll see that you get a decent burial," Landon promised.

"No. I wanna be cremated," Brad said.

"I'm sure Stush'll be willing to take care of that," Landon said.

Then, with tears streaming down his cheeks, Chris picked up his rifle and used it like a crutch to hobble back to his wheelchair. He sat down heavily because of his lack of legs, squirmed his ass and hips into the seat to get as comfortable as he could get, wiped his tears with his left hand, then lifted his rifle with the butt firmly pressed into his right shoulder. He waited for Brad to squirm around and come "back to life." Then he took careful aim, and blasted his friend Brad in the head.

CHAPTER 16

Cy-Fi and Oscar on my Podcast

John Russo and I had my niece and nephew as special guests on my third podcast, and I must say they acquitted themselves very well. John and I asked questions to prod them along and keep it lively. Again, in this transcript, he's **JR** and I'm **UJ**. Cy-Fi is **CF** and Oscar is **OS**. Cy-Fi was irrepressible, as usual, and she had rehearsed at home with Oscar so that he would come across more articulately than was normally possible for him, which I admit was something of a "cheat."

JR: Welcome to Uncle John's Podcast! We're pleased to have so many of you regularly tuning in. Today he and I are joined by his niece Cy-Fi and his nephew Oscar. To start out, we want to correct a misconception that still flourishes in some people's minds, even though it makes no chronological sense. Let's hopefully settle it once and for all. Oscar, please tell everybody if you have any memories of those infamous days back in the sixties when the first zombie epidemic broke out and was chronicled in the classic movie *Night of the Living Dead.*

OS: My mind is a blank about all that. I wasn't even born yet.

JR: Well, how old are you now, Oscar?

OS: How old am I, Sis?

CF: Thirty-three on your last birthday, in March.

OS: I keep forgetting.

JR: The first epidemic happened fifty years ago, so you'd have been minus-23 years old to have been there -- you'd have been not even an embryo yet!

CF: And not a viable human being! Except to the people who believe that embryos have Constitutional rights!

JR: Let's let that particular argument go for now. How are the two of you holding up under the pressure of your uncle's fame? You go first, Oscar.

OS: It's a pain in the butt sometimes. I can't even go get a Slurpy without bein' hounded by paparazzi.

JR: And it'll probably get worse after you've been on this podcast. You remind me of Fredo, Michael Corleone's brother, in that you don't seem to get the respect you deserve. But of course he was a little squirrelly guy, and you're big and strong looking. How does Uncle John treat you when the world isn't watching?

OS: Nobody better ever talk bad about him when *I'm* around!

JR: I'm sure of that, Oscar. Fredo wasn't loyal like you, he was a jealous type. He turned on Michael. He was easily co-opted by people smarter than he was.

OS: What's *co-opted* mean, Sis?

CF: Turned traitor. Which is something you'd never do, Bro.

UJ: Oscar would give his life to protect me. Which is something I hope he'll never have to do. But there are lots of people out to get me, and that's not paranoia, that's pure fact. As you well know, this podcast gets hundreds of hateful emails each and every week.

CF: I just delete them all. There's no use in keeping them, clogging up my computer and making me depressed.

JR: What about that, Cy-Fi? Tell us how close you are to Uncle John.

CF: We have a very loving relationship. He used to push me on the swings when I was a little kid. And then, after our parents died in a car accident, he adopted me and Oscar and treated us like his own, even though his wife left him because of it -- she thought he was paying more attention to us than to her, which wasn't true, it was in her mind.

UJ: Not only that, but she was a hoarder. She had so much junk it was driving us out of our home. So I wasn't unhappy to see her go. I called the Salvation Army and had them come and take all her junk away. It filled two dump trucks.

CF: She was mean to me and Oscar when you weren't around. One time she wanted to make us eat salt -- and I dumped it on her head. Then we ran off and hid in the woods for a day, till you came home. I forget what she was going to punish us for, but it was something we didn't even do.

JR: Do you and Oscar ever hear from her anymore?

CF: She came to my store and brought us a couple of presents. Trying to smooth-talk us because she knows we have money now. I told her to shove those gifts up her ass.

JR: I guess I don't blame you for that. I know that about half the world hates you. But are there those who want to be your pals?

CF: Well, yeah, but it's hard to trust any of them. They mostly want our money. They come to us with crazy schemes and crackpot inventions.

UJ: We've become targets for swindlers, just like the lottery winners.

OS: I liked the one guy with the car polish, though. According to him I'd never have to wax the Le Mans, ever again. You just rub it on and the shine lasts forever, he said.

CF: Oh, you're too gullible, Oscar!

JR: Are there any decent projects that you've actually invested in?

CF: Well, yes, there's Zombie Lube, researched and developed by us, in conjunction with Dr. Delbert Strange and his team at the Zombie Research Institute. It does away with erectile dysfunction. One hundred percent effective. We've had zero complaints. It's in all the stores now, even online. And we have a healthy share of the profits.

JR: Anything else that you can claim as a success? How about you, Oscar? Got any favorites?

OS: I like the Cold Crypt Pilsner. It's my favorite beer now.

JR: I enjoy it, too. In fact a little too much. But what can I say? I've always been a party guy. But I don't let it interfere with my work.

CF: You're doing a good job on the book so far. I read the first draft of everything up to today.

JR: Thank you. I'd like to hear more about some of the whacky schemes you've been hit with. Does anything stand out, Uncle John?

UJ: Yes. One fellow wanted to start a company to try to discover what makes zombies not be entirely dead. He was a scientist studying ways to prolong the human lifespan. He said he was into cryogenics before *we* came along, in other words the practice of freezing dead people in liquid helium so they can be thawed out maybe years and years from now, when we have a cure for whatever killed them -- but of course we'd also have to know how to cure the damaged done by freezing. He believes that zombies might embody the secret to eternal life. He said that if I wouldn't invest in his research, he'd go to the federal government, because our military would have a very good use for soldiers who couldn't be killed unless a bullet struck them in the head.

JR: Sounds like something our current President might approve of. They would be cheap, long-lasting recruits. And he could use the savings to give a huge tax break to the top one percent.

CF: Oh my God! Don't talk like that! You're scaring me!

UJ: It's a frightening thing to have to think about. He could use his trained zombie shoulders to come after people like me. Then when we were all taken care of, he could have them court-martialed and killed. I'm afraid I wouldn't put it past him.

On that happy note we signed off on the podcast. We didn't know it would be our last one, because of the plot that was in the works, against us.

***

Stush Polanski was having himself a bit of fun, all by himself in front of the cage, poking at the zombies with a long bamboo pole, making them hiss and growl because they couldn't get to him.

He put the pole down when he heard motorcycle sounds. He knew that his nephew was coming to see him, and he didn't always like for people to witness the dire depths of his sadism.

It could make them too wary of him when he had to sucker them into something -- like often their own death.

The motorcycle rider zoomed right up to Stush and dismounted, then took off his helmet with the dark visor. It was Steve Munch from FLSH-TV. He was Stush's nephew, and very few people knew that. He gave his gangster uncle a fist-bump and a bear hug.

Munch said, "Good to see ya, Unk!"

"You bangin' Mandy yet?" Stush asked.

"I *been* bangin' her, but don't spread it around. They've got a dumb saying at the station: Don't put your peter in the payroll."

"That's a hot one! Bet it don't stop anyone from gettin' in anybody's pants. You bonin' Mandy or not?"

"Yeah, I told you. Talk about hot ones, *she's* the hot one. A great conniver, too. She's gonna seduce Oscar and find out where they keep Uncle John. Then we can kidnap him for sure, Unk!"

"Does your boss at the station know I'm your uncle?"

"No, nobody's wise. Nobody that counts anyways. Uncle John is so damned famous you can charge your zombie hunters at least ten grand apiece for the thrill of going after him and getting him in their sights. I want twenty percent, ten percent of it for Mandy. She and I are splitting our take fifty-fifty ."

"Well, I don't wanna have to charge a slew of hunters to be in on it, even though they'd all like to. It'd call too much attention to us. I think I can get at least five of my big fat-cats to ante up a hundred grand each for the privilege of tryin' to bag Uncle John. Five times a hundred large is half a mil -- plus we'll shoot video and sell maybe a million bucks worth of DVD's -- if the FBI don't catch us, and I don't think they will."

Munch's eyes lit up and he said, "My twenty percent comes out of the whole take, from all sources, including the DVD market -- right Uncle Stush?"

"You got it, Stevie."

They gave each other another knuckle-bump and bear hug, and Munch hopped on his motorcycle and roared off.

Stush watched him go. And he had a sneaky grin on his face. Because he already knew how he was going to take care of his nephew so he wouldn't have to pay him.

***

Two nights later, Mandy Frost approached Oscar outside of a Uni-Mart where he had bought a Slurpy and a bag of cheese curls. "Oh my gosh, it's Oscar!" she said, feigning surprise. "I was trying to phone you, but I didn't have your number."

"Uh...what'd you want, Mandy?" Oscar stammered.

She lowered her voice, saying, "I want to interview you in private, without your sister. I'm much more interested in you than I am in her, but she never lets me get close to you. She always has to be around, hogging the limelight."

"Uh...my sister's not like that," Oscar protested a bit weakly. The truth was that he actually did have a bigger ego than most people suspected, and so he was as flattered as Mandy hoped he'd be by her overt come-on.

"I know you don't want to believe it," she said. "But she's taking advantage of you, playing you for a sucker." This was a lie, but she thought she could talk Oscar into swallowing it. She ran her hands over his chest, and he stood there staring down at her caressing hands, holding his Slurpy and his bag of cheese curls and once again turning beet red, as he had done at the press conference. His fingers were freezing from the ice-cold Slurpy but he found that he was paralyzed and couldn't do anything about it. Couldn't set it down and couldn't drink from it, even though his throat had gone totally dry.

"I'd like to *interview* you at my apartment," Mandy murmured with throaty, whispery suggestiveness.

Oscar let her lead him away, and they drove there in her car, a sporty little Mazda.

He was overwhelmed. He was like a gawky teenager on his first date. And he couldn't believe the implications of how she had spoken to him. Could it be that she actually liked him?

Could it be that he was about to lose his virginity? No! He couldn't be that lucky.

He found himself sitting next to Mandy in her living room, softly lit by a shaded lamp on an end table. And on the coffee table in front of them was a bottle of Chianti and two goblets.

Mandy poured, smiled at him and clinked his glass with hers, and she sipped but he kept staring at her without sipping. So she leaned forward and kissed him lightly on his lips, feigning shyness to an extent. Then she back away and said, "Oscar...why don't you take off that big clunky gun and holster? It's going to get in our way."

"Uh...okay...if you say so, Mandy."

He got up and started unbuckling his gun belt.

She said, Why don't you use the bathroom and freshen up, too. Meantime I'll get into something more comfortable."

He eyed her, dumbfounded.

"The bathroom's over there, Oscar," she told him, pointing the way.

He went down the hall, and she quickly took a little vial of white powder out of her purse, dumped it into his wine and stirred it. Then she hustled into her bedroom, took off her street clothes and slipped into a filmy negligee.

When he came out of the bathroom, to her surprise he must have dumped some of his shyness. Because he was no longer wearing his uniform shirt and his gun. Instead he was down to his wife-beater undershirt. She thought it all went to show what lust can do to a guy, even a shy one like him, with a huge inferiority complex. And she was flattered that the lust had been inspired by her.

She motioned for him to sit beside her again, on the couch. And she lifted his goblet of wine to his lips and coaxed him to drink it all. Then she got up and turned on some music, an up-tempo number suitable for a striptease, and she began dancing front of him and slowly taking off her bra, her panties, and then her negligee.

She was doing all this to give the drug she had given him enough time for it to work.

He watched her, google-eyed.

Then she sat in his lap and kissed him.

In a little while he told her everything she needed to know.

CHAPTER 17

My Brain Storms

Dr. Strange had me take a battery of psychological tests to try to find out if zombies think like regular people to any great extent and if my own particular brain behaved differently in ways that might be measurable. "We've studied them with brain scans," he said to me. "But you're one of the rare ones who can talk intelligently. Therefore it could be vastly beneficial for us to glean your insights."

I ventured to tell him that I had long speculated that the zombie disease might be somehow a mutated combination of multiple sclerosis and Alzheimer's, the former impairing the body and the latter impairing the brain. The horror of Alzheimer's, as I understand it, is that you can feel your mind slipping away from you. And that is exactly what I experienced in the first stages. But luckily the process gradually stopped, in my case, and began to reverse itself. All sufferers should be so lucky. I dearly hoped that by working with me they way they wanted to, Dr. Strange and his colleagues at the Zombie Research Institute could discover something helpful.

They administered a Rorschach test, a Minnesota Multiphasic Personality Inventory, and a raft of other gobbledygook that I don't remember the names of. I guess a lot of folks would just call it psychobabble. But nevertheless the scientists got excited. The results indicated to them that my mind as well as my body had been affected in strange ways by the zombie disease. I was a unique zombie, they said. And I supposed that I should take that as a compliment.

One of the issues they were trying to settle was whether or not the Undead had any deep thoughts about the things they were compelled to do. For instance, did they feel any pangs of conscience? Or were they solely driven by the part of the brain known as the Reptile Complex, the primitive part, the seat of the blind, relentless urge to kill and eat?

On the other hand, did they retain some of the mammalian part of the brain, the seat of empathy and caring? If so, did *all* zombies share those kinds of feelings, or only the ones like me who had somehow regained the ability to talk and make sense? Was it possible that the speech function was somehow enigmatically tied to the ability to feel empathy?

I assured them that I personally possessed a deep empathy for all creatures, including humans. It was why I didn't just attack and devour people indiscriminately. Instead I made moral judgments. It was what I *had* to do in order to believe that I had a right to go on living. I didn't like the state I was in, but I wanted to ameliorate it as much as possible.

Judging purely by the *behavior* of the Undead ones who could *not* talk, I think that they did not substantially possess the finer qualities that I have alluded to. They seemed to me to be little different from hungry reptiles who would mindlessly devour their own young. When I had a choice, I would choose to hang out with the more intellectual ones. But I was like that even before I turned into a zombie. My closest friends, the ones I gravitated to, were eagerly attuned to the arts, politics and the humanities.

Even back then, my thinking on most subjects was unorthodox, but I think extremely valid even though not readily accepted by most people. I have always been a person who thinks "outside the box." I even had a chapter called that in my book *The Death of Our Democracy: An American Horror Story*. I will present here some excerpts from the Outside the Box chapter. I must say that I personally don't find some of these ideas terribly far-out or farfetched. Some of them might actually work if they were put into practice. I've been thinking about them lately. I went back and revisited them, thinking to bring them up on my podcast. I hoped to provoke an intense discussion and garner some feedback -- but, as I said, the plot that was brewing against me caused the podcast to be aborted after only three broadcasts. And so, I would love to hear what *you* think. You will find my email address at: myunclejohnisazombie.com.

The Legislative Lottery

What if we selected one-third of every legislature, local, state and national, by lottery -- the same way we select juries?

Our elected representatives are supposed to always act in our best interests, but it often seems that they seldom or never do. Democracy was founded on the idea that everyone should have a voice, yet according to noted historian Simon Goldhill, "Nothing frightens modern democracies so much as the specter of popular participation."

Why are they frightened? Don't they want anyone to see what they are doing?

I don't think that the common citizen would do a worse job than many of the scoundrels who spend millions of donor dollars to stay in office and get rich. In fact, if they weren't so beholden to wealthy benefactors, they might use their best judgment about what is good for *us* instead of what is good for *them*.

Perhaps more importantly, if the average person knew he had a chance to actually *serve* in government one day, knowledge of that chance might engender a great upsurge of interest and appreciation of the workings of our system -- and greater voter participation. Soon everybody would know a friend, a family member or a guy down the street who was serving or had served in congress! The talk around the kitchen table and in bars, restaurants and beauty parlors might make an inroad into the usual inane gossip and prattle about sports, hair styles and diets. And the people already holding office would have watchdogs and whistle blowers looking over their shoulders. They would become more fearful of being undone by their own dishonesty or their own secretly-held sexual peccadilloes.

How Television Corrupts Politics

TV advertising is the main reason why it costs so much to get elected these days. In Abe Lincoln's day a candidate would go by horse and buggy from town to town, village to village, and get up on a stump and talk. But now there is little chance of winning a seat unless you can reach millions of people by television. And this costs millions and millions of dollars, usually provided by wealthy individuals and corporations. Candidates are obliged to spend most of their time raising money instead of doing the people's business. They are forever beholden to the fat-cats who backed them.

I think that the solution might be to severely regulate and downsize the amount of money that is allowed to be spent by political campaigns on television. Maybe then we'd be cutting the problem off at its roots, like cutting off the supply illegal drugs by shooting the dealers instead of jailing the addicts.

Bringing Back the Stock and Pillory

Largely due to the criminalization of drug use, the United States has the largest prison population per capita in the so-called civilized world. As a result, the communities of poor and downtrodden no longer attach much stigma to persons who have done or are doing prison time. In fact, among many in such communities it's a badge of respect. They say, "You can't trust anybody who doesn't have ridges on his stomach."

So, what can we do to reform the situation?

We lament the use of the stock and pillory in olden times, but it did have one major

advantage: stigma. Public embarrassment. When you had your arms and legs clamped in those blocks of wood, you were at the mercy of anyone who passed by. They could pelt you with rotten eggs. They could stone you. They could even do deplorable things of a perverted sexual nature. I can't think of anybody who would like to be locked in a stock and pillory. But there are plenty of repeat offenders who don't seem to mind repetitive jail time. The popular idea of it is that all they do is pump iron, eat three square meals a day and watch television when they're not raping each other in the shower.

I think the stock and pillory should be tried out in Washington, D.C. it could be placed prominently on Capitol Hill, or else within view of the White House as a warning to its current occupant. He tweets nasty things about zombies almost every day now. Especially about me. Zombies can be scary, but they don't try to tear down the institutions of government that are the bulwark of our democracy.

Once again we should take a lesson from the past. After the assassination of Julius Caesar, when Mark Antony tried to gain control of Rome by telling Octavian that the senators would never support anyone so young and inexperienced, Octavian said simply, "I have an army."

That is exactly what the President has over us: an army of more than thirty million people who will stick with him no matter what he does. What he cares about, even more than getting re-elected is his base. His power. He's a ruthless opportunist, an unintended consequence, a natural progression in the degenerative debasement of his party. We should have seen it coming when George W. Bush openly said to his supporters at a $10,000-a-plate banquet, "You are my base -- the haves and the have mores." And, after that, when Mitt Romney was surreptitiously recorded saying what he really believed, that "forty-seven percent of the population of our country is made up of people who believe they are victims and are dependent upon the government." And even more recently, after he signed a tax bill that will kill the middle class and the poor, the Tweeter-in-Chief told a crowd of sycophants at his luxury resort, "You are about to get even richer." These people scare me much more than any zombie could, even if I weren't one.

CHAPTER 18

Jane's Informer

Pow! Pow! Pow! Rapid gunshots. After each one, the tinkle of tin hitting gravel.

Zeke Corrigan, one of Stush's hunters, was blasting away at beer cans, test-firing his new rifle. He was a big guy, six four, with a huge beer belly, a shaved head and long wild beard that would have suited the stars of *Duck Dynasty*.

Detective Jane Smart came up on him from behind and stood there with her fingers in her ears till he stopped shooting at the beer cans. Knowing that she was behind him all the while, he turned around and smirked at her, lecherously. He said, "Well, hello, sweetheart. Got my reward money?"

"You don't get a cent unless your information pans out, Zeke. And even then you don't get paid unless we get a conviction."

She was dealing with Zeke Corrigan now, because the undercover detective she had planted hadn't been heard from in a while, and she was pretty sure he must be dead.

With his rifle on a sling over his shoulder, Zeke reached into the right-hand front pocket of his Levis and unfolded a flier that said: $10,000 REWARD FOR INFORMATION ON ILLEGAL ZOMBIE HUNTING CAMPS! Then he said gruffly, "Before I rat the place out, I want a guarantee of immunity for all my crimes past or present. And I won't do nothin' in the way of cooperation till my lawyer approves the guarantee."

Jane expected him to demand no less than that. But his past crimes filled a rap sheet half a yard long, everything from kidnapping to armed robbery. And the way he got out of prison was by ratting out a cell mate. It made her sick to have to deal with him. But her job obliged her to deal with scum.

She said, "There were things you wouldn't cop to when you made the turncoat deal that got you out of the county jail. So now you have to own up to everything on your rap sheet. And don't think we're not wise to other things that didn't get on there for lack of proof. You have to go into all the missing details. But I hope we're not talking about murder here, because that would gum up the works."

"I ain't guilty of any murders, unless you think killin' zombies is a crime. Actually, I ain't killed that many -- I'm a lousy shot. I've been tryin' to get better at it by goin' out and shootin' at beer cans. I drink lotsa beer, so I've got plenty of cans for target practice. I wanna try that Cold Crypt beer that Uncle John's been ravin' about on TV."

"It's a pilsner. And I think he's a hoax. But let's not get off the subject. You've been a zombie hunter, and now you want to spill the beans on other hunters?"

"Fuck 'em. I hate the guy who runs the place, Stush Polanski. First off, I'm such a bad shot I don't make much in the way of prize money. And what I do make, he cheats me out of -- the sleazy sonofabitch!"

"Are you willing to wear a wire?"

Mulling it over, he said, "Yeah, I guess I'd take that chance -- if I could get half the ten thousand up front. And providin' I could be guaranteed a place in the Witness Protection Program, if I should ever need it. Stush hates snitches. He shoots 'em in the head without even thinkin' about it, as if they're no better than zombies."

"Hmmm," Jane said. "Tell me more of what you know about this bad ass, Stush Polanski. We already know a lot, but I'm sure we don't know as much as you do."

***

Later that day, after dark, Steve Munch rode his Harley to the hunting camp and pulled up by the big outdoor cage where Stush was once again tormenting the zombies by poking them with a long bamboo pole. This time he had dared to open the cage door so it was easier to poke the pole at them, but he kept his pistol handy, under his belt.

Munch got right to his main reason for being there. "You got my cash ready for me, Uncle Stush?"

"Don't worry," Stush assured him. "You're gonna get paid. Just gimme a chance to collect from some of the fat-cat hunters. They're always slow pay, don't like to cash in their stocks and bonds too soon while they're earnin' money for 'em."

"C'mon, don't you have a little on hand that you can give me to tide me over? Say five or ten thousand? I'm taking a hell of a chance helping you with this Uncle John scheme."

"For crissake, you're gonna *get* all your money. You're like a whiney little kid."

"I want some *now*, Uncle Stush! You always taught me not to take anyone at his word, not even you. All I want to do is make you proud."

"Okay," Stush said, clapping his nephew on the shoulder. "Let's go into the lodge where

the cash box is. You're a fart smeller, I mean a smart feller, right?"

They both laughed at the old joke.

Stush started to swing the cage door shut, then stopped. "Hey, wait a minute," he said. "I just noticed this door ain't hangin' right. The fuckin' zombies musta banged it up, screwed up the hinges. Gimme a hand with it, will ya?"

"Sure, Uncle Stush."

"Swing it back and forth a few times. Maybe it needs some oil."

Munch started doing it, then said, "It doesn't seem like there's anything wrong with it, Uncle Stush."

Stush shoved him into the cage, then slammed the door shut with a loud clang and securely locked it.

The hungry zombies started closing in on Munch. He cried out, "Please, let me out! Don't let me die like this!"

Stush chortled and stepped close to the wire mesh, ready to enjoy the fun.

Munch screamed, "My Harley! You gotta let me go! The cops're gonna find it! You'll never get away with this!"

The zombies started pulling Munch down, chomping into him.

Laughing sadistically, Stush said, "I'm gonna torch your fuckin' motorcycle! Take it into the woods and set on fire!"

He laughed even louder as his nephew was torn apart.

CHAPTER 19

Jane Smart's Change of Heart

Cy-Fi and I created a Political Action Committee, *Send a Zombie to Congress*, because we could no longer sit silently on the sidelines listening to the lies coming out of Congress and the White House. They really got our hackles up when they rushed through a package they called "Budget Reform" which was really a budget deformity that gave away billions of dollars to the wealthiest people in America by raping the middle class and the poor.

The mid-term elections coming up were of monumental importance to the future of our democracy. Cy-Fi and I strongly believed that zombies had to band together with other concerned citizens to stop our slide into the repressively autocratic brand of government that the Executive Branch was perpetrating.

Send a Zombie to Congress was a grass-roots endeavor with a vital purpose. My niece and I launched it by publishing an op-ed on the back page of the front section of the *Pittsburgh Tribune Review*. It took up the whole page. Here is an extract:

ZOMBIES AND CITIZENS RISE UP!

We exhort all people, dead and undead, to band together to rescue our republic! Our government is not working "for the people" and we need to change that for the good of all -- the rich, the poor and the in-between.

Flesh-eating ghouls are no longer just the simple-minded critters that people came to know and fear back in the sixties. Some of us nowadays are not stupid, not totally brain dead; in fact, we can be a lot smarter than many so-called "normal" folks out there who put zombies down and consider themselves superior.

Tired of being mocked, tired of being shot at, tired of seeing this country operated for the few instead of the many, zombies are going after the fat cats who have engorged themselves on the nation's wealth. These highly principled zombies long to dine on the chubby flesh of greedy, self-serving lobbyists and hypocritical legislators.

Insensitive political and cultural analysts express befuddlement over their belated realization that flesh-eating zombies, in spite of their unusual predilections, can actually be capable of making intelligent choices when it comes to national issues. But they should've wised up before now -- the clues were always there for the observant among us.

The collapse of our economy, the depletion of our military, and the destruction of the middle class did not happen overnight. It took decades of stupidity and greed. We all need to stop it and make sure it never happens again.

Writer/director George A. Romero has explored the evolution of zombies into intelligent

beings. In his early work they wielded clubs and rocks. But in his later movies they behaved a lot like regular people, for instance ransacking and hiding out in a mall, raising as much havoc as hordes of people do on the day after Thanksgiving, as if they retained an innately atavistic memory of their forfeited place in the trashy, over-commercialized society they had grown up in. One of them, in LAND OF THE DEAD, even took a stab at playing a trombone whose shiny brass had caught his eye!

If these zombies' rotting hearts are in the right place, shouldn't yours be? Shouldn't you

be helping them to drive the fat cats out of Washington? Shouldn't you be helping us promote our liberal agenda?

You don't have to be a zombie to join our PAC. Check out our web site. There are lots

of things zombies can't do on their own. They desperately need the help of every noble, highly concerned American.

So, send a zombie to Congress -- where he can find something good and proper to chew on!

Our op-ed created quite a furor. For days, the President kept tweeting about it, babbling that we were no better than the football players who were "taking a knee" when the National Anthem was being sung. He said they should all be locked up in Guantanamo and I should be shot on sight.

One evening while I was watching the coverage we were getting on MSNBC, Cy-Fi barged in on me, all excited. "I've been going through a ton of emails!" she blurted. "And guess what -- there's one from that detective!"

"Jane Smart?" I said, dumbfounded. "What on earth could she want?"

"She wants to join our PAC! She made a donation -- put it on a charge card."

"How much?"

"Two hundred bucks. That can't be easy on a cop's salary."

"That's true. They ought to be paid better."

"She says she agrees with a lot of the points we made in our op-ed. She wants to meet with you in person."

"Should I do it?"

"I think you should avoid her like the plague. She's probably trying to wheedle her way in with us so she can snoop around. She still wants to nail us for Clyde Yancey."

But I couldn't help it, I was intrigued. I asked Cy-Fi to email Jane back and try to set up a meeting someplace where Jane couldn't easily do me harm. I felt like Michael Corleone agreeing to meet with that sly, evil drug czar, Sillozzo.

The meeting took place on a Friday evening in October at an Italian restaurant called Pasquale's in downtown Pittsburgh. It had checkered tablecloths and Chianti bottles with wax candles in them. Cy-Fi rode me there in the Le Mans and dropped me off while she parked it in a pay-by-the-hour garage across the street. I waited for her on the sidewalk before going in. Jane was sitting at a table by herself with a menu and a glass of red wine in front of her. Cy-Fi took a seat three tables away so she could keep an eye out for trouble, but not close enough to eavesdrop and Jane would realize that.

"I'm glad you came," Jane said.

"Why? Are you going to arrest me?"

"No. I don't go back on my promises."

"So why are you being suddenly so nice to me? And why did you join our Political Action Committee?"

"You have some very good unusual ideas. I have to admit it. And as they say, politics makes strange bedfellows."

I perked up. Was she hinting that she actually might go to bed with me?

"Don't take me literally," she said. "I can see the wheels turning and I know how your dirty mind works."

"Dirty?"

"Don't worry, I'm not sexually repressed," she said with a mischievous smirk. "Except where zombies are concerned."

I knew that if the two of us ever hooked up it'd be a real Beauty and the Beast kind of thing. But I wasn't going to stop trying. I still had the hots for her.

"Do you want to order some wine? Or some dinner? Something to snack on?" Jane asked me.

"I can't enjoy it so much anymore. My taste buds are half dead. And I used to be a pasta freak, but now it doesn't agree with me anymore."

"I'm sorry to hear that. I guess you miss out on a lot."

She actually had a sympathetic look on her face, for a fleeting moment at least, and I saw her hand jerk as if she almost wanted to reach out to me. I think we both felt awkward in each other's company. Even though she had joined my PAC, I still needed to find out how much of an

enemy she was still going to be. As if she had read my mind on that subject, she said, "I must tell you, I'm not going to stop my investigation of you and your niece and nephew. But in the meantime, I think I can be objective enough to support your political aims. I'd like to help you bring down the Tweeter in Chief. He's an embarrassment both here and abroad. He's dragging this country down, brazenly ignoring the emoluments clause and using his presidency to enrich himself at everybody else's expense."

"You certainly sound as if you're passionately against him."

"I certainly *am*."

"Great, you're a thoughtful person. What're your thoughts about how you can be a productive member of our Zombie PAC? I mean, besides the money you pitched in."

"Well, you probably already know that most cops aren't liberals. I'm a rarity in that regard, maybe because I'm a female. I'm the only woman in the Detective Division. I take a lot of flak aimed at my gender as well as my political views. The guys I have to work with are a bunch of knuckle-dragging sexists. They brag endlessly about finally having one of their own in the White House. I used to ask them how they could be stupid enough to vote for a narcissist and congenital liar, but they ganged up on me and called me a dumb dyke -- and I'm not either. They think all tree huggers, immigrant coddlers and zombie-sympathizers should be caged or shot."

"You sure don't seem like a zombie sympathizer to me, Jane. You've been bound and determined to do away with me any way you can."

"But I still empathize with you and anybody else who comes down with that disease. It's just that I can't allow you to go on eating the kinds of things that you say you like to eat. But you've got a pretty strong base of supporters going for you due to your notoriety, your web site, your podcasts, and now your op-ed and your PAC." She made her points with great intensity, biting her lip and brushing back her golden hair in between thoughts, and I found her to be not only intelligent but quite charming.

"I'll do anything you ask me to do," she said. "I'll stuff envelopes, lick stamps, make phone calls and go door to door. No task is too small. We've got to get that tyrant out of the White House!"

"I agree with you, that's for sure, Jane. But how do I know you're not just trying to get close to me so you can bring *me* down?"

"Because you're so high-profile right now. And I'm under scrutiny by my fellow cops. Some of them would dearly love to see me bounced off the force. If I did anything stupid, like planting evidence or something, they'd gloat and rat me out, figuring two birds got killed with one stone. The commissioner would come down on me hard and my career would be over. I'd probably do jail time. So I'm not making an easy choice here."

"You sound sincere," I told her. "Let me talk this over with Cy-Fi and we'll get back to you."

"By the way," she said, "do you know anything about what may have happened to Sheriff McClelland? He's an *ex*-sheriff but I still call him that. He was still on the job when my father was a cop. He started out under him as a patrolman."

"Your father was a cop? Is he still alive?"

"No, luckily he didn't live to see what happened to my mother."

"I saw you telling about it on TV. My condolences, Jane."

"Thank you."

"Why are you asking me about that old sheriff?"

"He didn't show up for his bail hearing. He was indicted for shooting that black guy -- what's-his-name, Ben?"

"In the first zombie outbreak? That was fifty years ago."

"Yeah, but the ACLU thinks he shot the poor man on purpose, under the pretense that he was just another zombie. But I know the sheriff from when my dad worked for him, and I don't believe he'd do anything like that. I was going to be a character witness if he was put on trial."

"Are you sure you're on the level with me, Detective Smart? You've been on me about Clyde Yancey. Maybe now you think I did something to the old sheriff. And we both know what that something would be."

"Well, you can't blame me for asking, can you? Maybe he just skipped bail, but I find that hard to believe because he was so intent on clearing his name. I'm scared something bad might've happened to him."

"Well, I had nothing to do with it, Jane."

CHAPTER 20

Oscar and I Get Drunk

One afternoon Oscar drove me to a university campus in the Oakland section of Pittsburgh, where I delivered a talk at the Student Union. It was a lively and attentive audience and there were very good follow-up questions from the students and their professors. I was keyed-up by it, and after one of these events, which take a lot out of me, I have a need to wind down.

I coaxed Oscar into taking me to a campus bar called Jimbo's where I recalled that crowds of students used to hang out. It was pretty much the way I remembered it, except now there was the ubiquitous use of cell phones. The shoulder-to-shoulder young people at the bar and at the tables reminded me of pumpkins, the way their faces were lit up in the orange glow of dim, smoke-filled lighting and the glowing screens of their phones. Their fingers never ceased

their spider-like crawling over the little buttons, making wonder if massive cases of carpal tunnel syndrome were in the offing.

People weren't relating to each other, but to their phones. Wasn't it bad enough that they stared at screens all day in their homes and workplaces? Did they have to carry the practice into their supposedly leisure time? Didn't they ever want to *not* communicate with anybody?

It was a good thing Cy-Fi wasn't there to rain on my parade because suddenly I felt like getting half-plastered, and she would've put the kibosh on it. I figured I deserved to hang loose and have some fun once in a while. I thought of something I used to get a kick out of that an old alcoholic friend of mine used to say: "If you get drunk and don't make an ass of yourself, you're wasting your money."

Oscar was ready and willing to aid and abet. We started off by pounding down a couple shots of tequila. Then we each did a third round, clinking our glasses together and slamming them down empty. Oscar got into a coughing fit, but I didn't. I suppose that not only my vocal chords but also other parts of my throat weren't as sensitive as Oscar's.

The bartender put two more shots of tequila in front us that somebody else had bought, and we looked all around but couldn't figure out who. Then two college kids came over to us, a boy and a girl wearing cut-off jeans and University of Pittsburgh jerseys, and both swaying and slurring, half tipsy. They looked to be about nineteen or twenty, but they had to have been 21 or older since they would've been carded at the door. I was even carded but allowed to come in, in spite of the bruising and rotting on my face. I think barely gave me a glance, just checked my ID. Halloween was only a couple of weeks away, so maybe that helped.

The boy said, "We bought you the drinks."

And the girl said, "I'm Amy, and he's my boyfriend, Jeff."

She suddenly stopped swaying, stared at me hard, and said, "Hey, aren't you the zombie

Russo   page 130

they call Uncle *John?*"

"Oh boy, yeah, you're him for *sure!*" Jeff enthused. "Don't try to say you're not, because we sure as shit recognize you from TV!"

"I keep hoping my complexion will clear up so I can go incognito," I murmured drily.

Amy giggled and said, "That's *funny!*"

Jeff giggled along with her.

I started singing, "Amy, Amy, give me your answer do, I'm half-crazy all for the lover of you..."

Jeff said, "Hey! *He* can sing!"

Amy said, "We knew you could talk, Uncle John, but we didn't know you can *sing!* You ought to sing something on television!"

113

Flattered and pretty drunk, I sang some more. "It won't be a stylish marriage, I can't afford a carriage! But you'll look sweet upon the seat, of a bicycle built for two!"

Jeff and Amy burst into drunken applause, and Oscar clapped along with them.

Jeff said, "Pretty good, but that song's got to be about two hundred years old! Can me and Amy have your autograph?"

Amy said, "It doesn't have to be on a glossy photo or anything. Just on a bar napkin. Pretty please?"

"We promise not to sell it on eBay," Jeff added.

I told them, "I wouldn't care what you did with it. Once I gave it to you, it'd be totally yours to do with it as you pleased. But I'm afraid I can't sign anything. I have too much leftover rigor mortis in my fingers."

"Aw...that's too bad," Amy said sadly.

And Jeff said, "Let us buy you another shot." He motioned for the bartender, who came over and poured refills. We clinked glasses all around and tossed down the tequila.

I was drunk enough to tell one of my favorite old jokes. "What do you get when you cross a donkey with an onion?"

Amy stated laughing before I even got to the punch line. Jeff just stood there weaving a little and waiting to hear it.

I said, "A piece of ass so good it brings tears to your eyes."

"Uncle *John!*" Amy moaned. But she was still laughing.

"There you go talkin' dirty again," Oscar drawled. "Good thing Cy-Fi ain't here."

CHAPTER 21

I Get Kidnapped

Grandpa's birthday was coming up that October, and he would've been 83 years old, except he had been dead for 18 years. He was actually *my* grandfather and Oscar and Cy-Fi's great-grandfather. He wasn't any prize package either. He was an abusive alcoholic. He never worked a regular job; instead he gave cheap haircuts, seating people in an old barber chair in his cellar, with stuffing coming out of its cracked red leather seat. He only charged fifty cents per haircut, but he wasn't a very good barber so his customers were mostly kids sent to him by their mothers after they would first check to see if he happened to be sober that week. The kids all got haircuts that looked as if he had put a bowl over their heads. Luckily my mom wouldn't let me be one of his victims. He wouldn't drive when he was drunk; instead he would call a taxi. He fell getting out of a cab one day and it ran over his left leg, which had to be amputated. He was even less stable after that, which led to a second fall, this time in traffic, whereby he lost his right leg; so he ended up with two artificial limbs, but that didn't stop his drinking binges. He died by hitting his head when he fell trying to get up from a bar stool.

Cy-Fi wanted me and Oscar to rake leaves around Grandpa's grave and put down some plastic flowers. I saw no sense in any of it, when you're dead you're dead, but nevertheless we went to the cemetery to do the job. We were also hung over because it was the day after our drinking binge with the two college students.

There were so many maple leaves all over the ground that I was pretty tired raking them and Oscar wouldn't take a turn at it because he said I needed the exercise to tamp down my rigor mortis. That was always Oscar's excuse when he wanted me to do all the work. This time he also said he would puke if he had to handle a rake.

I said, "Why do we have to keep raking these damned leaves anyhow, Oscar? The wind keeps blowing them back where I already raked!"

"Because we're making it nice for Grandpa. He's up in heaven lookin' down on us."

"I thought he was under that gravestone." I was toying with Oscar, just to get him befuddled.

"Well, he *is* under it -- but he *ain't*. His body's under it, but his soul's up in heaven. With God and his son Jesus Christ."

"How do we know that, Oscar?" I was playing dumb just to see what he would say. I also didn't believe in what he was saying.

"I was taught it in Sunday School. We have to believe it 'cause it's in the bible. And it makes us feel good."

"Well," I said, "it doesn't make *me* feel good. I'm damned tired of raking. How could he have got up to heaven on two plastic legs?"

"He musta been pulled up through the clouds just like an angel," Oscar said. "God don't care what you look like when you get there. He fixes everything that happens to be wrong with ya."

I gave a vicious pull on the rake and accidentally ran it through the plastic flowers, ripping some of them out of their flimsy little paper pots.

Oscar said, "Oh, shucks, Uncle John! You ruined 'em! I'll have to get another two from the car trunk. " He headed back toward the Le Mans and I wiped sweat from my brow. A lot of zombies that I knew didn't sweat, but I was one who did. Maybe because I did a lot more heavy work than some of the more primitive ones did.

Meanwhile, Oscar and I were unaware that two of Stush's thugs had sneaked into the cemetery. It was Joe Talerico and another guy called Blue, who sported a big beer belly and a bucket-sized shaved head. He was wearing a red T-shirt and a leather vest. Joe, a lot lankier, was wearing the same black hoodie he wore when he helped kidnap that girl, Betty, in the yellow bikini, at her daddy's lakeside cottage.

Blue hoisted a Coleman cooler out of Joe's van. He banged it too hard setting it down,

and Joe said, "Not so loud! Don't wanna shake him up and get bit. Even if we *don't* get bit, we might get shot."

"By who?" Blue asked with a blank look on his unshaven face. He was like Oscar when it came to brain power; not the brightest bulb in the chandelier. That's a trite way of saying it, but I like sayings like that: Two bricks shy of a load or two french-fries short of a Happy Meal.

"By his dumbass nephew, Oscar. As a bodyguard he sucks, but he can pull a trigger. At least Cy-Fi won't be around to fuck us up. Mandy got her out of our hair by havin' her come to the TV studio to sign a fat contract -- which she'll never collect on, if everything goes our way."

"I wouldn't mind bangin' her. I seen her on TV."

"So did the whole world."

"The whole world banged her?" Blue said, leering lecherously.

"No. Just the whole world seen her on TV."

"Oh," Blue said, disappointed.

"You got that fresh hand and forearm?"

"Got it right here in the cooler."

Joe said, "I hear the cannibals in Africa like the palms of folks's hands. To them they're a delicacy."

"Yuck! Not in *my* stomach," Blue said.

"Tie the monofilament onto it, I don't wanna touch it," said Joe. "We harvested it from a guy we had to kill. He was gonna rat us out to the cops, but we turned him into zombie feed."

I had resumed raking leaves and was waiting for Oscar to come back with more plastic flowers. I didn't see Joe toss the severed hand and forearm out in my direction, from his hiding place behind a tombstone. And my eyes weren't sharp enough to spot the monofilament that he used to drag it toward him as soon as it caught my attention. At first I didn't see it, I just smelled it. Like all zombies I can smell a fresh morsel from a short distance away, and I stopped raking and sniffed the air.

I saw the hand lying in the grass and dropped the rake and went toward it -- but Joe pulled it away from me.

I stooped and made a grab at it and Joe yanked it again.

I wanted it badly at this point and, blinded by hunger, I never spotted the monofilament. I don't think anybody would have, not even regular people with decent eyesight. It was almost invisible winding through the grass. I was always alert to the smell of fresh human meat, and they were using that against me. The more I sniffed it, the more I was enticed by it and kept after it, but Joe kept pulling it away from me. Finally he got me lured me to the edge of a gravel access road. He let me stoop and grab the tasty prize and start munching on it for a second or two -- and that's the precise moment that they tossed a burlap sack over my head, wrapped me up with rope, and dumped me into the back of Joe's van. Just before they slammed the back door shut, I heard Oscar yell and fire off several shots, which was dumb, because one of them nearly hit me when it made a hole in the van.

The vehicle peeled out with a loud screech, tossing me around in there like a big sack of potatoes.

I was bound up in there, bouncing roughly around, for about a half hour, I believe, but I don't have such a great sense of time passage any more. Finally the van screeched to a halt and Joe and Blue opened the cargo door, dragged me out and got me on my feet, still tied up in the burlap sack.

I heard Joe say, "Wait a minute, let me get hold of a cattle prod."

I thought, Oh-oh, what the hell are they gonna *do* to me? If they were planning on torturing me, I couldn't figure out why. Of course evil people like that don't need a reason, they can just do it to have fun.

They didn't untie the sack till they carried me bodily into the hunting lodge. Before it was lifted off of me I heard Stush's voice for the first time saying, "Don't take the sack all the way off till you zap him a few times so he knows what it feels like. Do it, Joe."

I heard the zap and immediately felt the pain. I thought I could even smell the burlap burning. I yelled, "*Ow!* Damn it!" He zapped me a few more times and I kept squirming and yelling -- *Ow! Ow! Ow!* -- in rhythm with the prods.

Stush said, "We're gonna remove the burlap sack, but if you act up you'll get more of the same."

I certainly didn't want any more of that, so I said, "Okay...*okay!* Who're *you* and what do you *want?*"

"That's for me to know and you to find out, Mr. Brain Dead. And if you bite me, I'll just shoot you in the head and be done with it."

"If I bite you, you'll be done for, too. I mean in your present form."

"I won't get close enough for you to do that," said Stush. "And I'll keep my gun aimed at your fuckin' head, smart-ass! So don't try anything funny."

I certainly didn't want to get shot in the head, so I said, "I promise not to bite any of you. Anyhow, I've already had my snack."

"What the fuck're you talkin' about? Take the sack off of him, Joe."

Blue and Joe tugged the sack over my head -- and they jumped back when they saw that I was munching on the severed arm and hand.

"Yuck!" Joe exclaimed. "He's been chewin' on the damn thing even while he's been tied up in the sack!"

"Well," I explained, "I already had it in my mouth when you dropped the sack over me.

So I figured I should make sure I had enough energy for whatever was gonna happen to me. But it was hard keeping it between my teeth to gnaw at without being able to use my hands because they were tied down at my sides."

"Well, excuse *me* for the inconvenience," Stush said. "Get him into the cage, Joe!"

"Wait a minute!" I said. I tried to take another bite out of my snack -- but Blue yanked at it, trying to take it away from me. A tug-of-war ensued, but he was stronger than I was and he finally grabbed it and tossed it to the floor.

Stush said, "I was gonna let you keep munchin' on that arm after we got you locked up, but now I'm not goin' to, Mr. Brain Dead!"

I said, "That's not very nice."

And he said, "Zap him a couple more times, Joe. Make him get in the special cage."

He wasn't referring to the big outdoor cage where they kept a dozen or more zombies at a time. This one was a much smaller cage on casters that could be rolled around from place to place, like the ones used to take dangerous prisoners into a courtroom for hearings and trials. That's what they shoved me into.

After the door banged shut, I became aware of a TV that was tuned to Faux News, my least favorite station. A talking head was lavishing undeserved praise on the President.

I took heart from the fact that I was being kept separate from the others. I deduced that maybe Stush didn't want me getting into any scraps, didn't want me damaged in any way. I must have a special value to him. Maybe he was going to hold me for ransom and I'd soon be out of there. Cy-Fi and my hordes of fans would surely pay any amount that was demanded of them, even if they had to run an Indiegogo campaign.

CHAPTER 22

Cy-Fi Gets the Bad News

Frantic and guilt-ridden, Oscar barged into the conference room at FLSH-TV where Cy-Fi was signing a long-term contract for me, her and Oscar. She was with the program director, Don Harvey, and they were affixing their signatures to the documents.

Cy-Fi said, "Oscar! You're interrupting a meeting! I told you to stay with Uncle John."

"He's been *kidnapped!*" he told her. "And it's my fault!"

"Omigod! How did it happen?"

"I left him alone for five minutes and he got jumped! I saw them speeding away from him in a van! I tried to shoot out the tires but it kept going!"

Poor Oscar. He was in a dither. He kept pacing around frantically while Cy-Fi tried to remain calm enough to think straight.

Don Harvey was rather merciless. He said, "If you don't get him back his contract is null and void and you're obligated to refund the advance."

He stomped out of the room and Cy-Fi gave him the finger behind his back.

Oscar was almost in tears. "Poor Uncle John," he lamented. "I'll never forgive myself if anything bad happens to him."

Cy-Fi seized the tabs of his shirt collar, pulled him to within inches of her face and stared him in the eyes. "Damn it, Oscar, pull yourself together and think!" she demanded. "Did you at least get the license plate number?"

"It was covered with mud."

"Oh, for God's sake!"

"I can't *help* it, Sis."

"I know...I know."

In despair, she yanked her cell phone out of her purse, punched in some numbers and looked relieved when the person she was calling answered. "Hello, Detective Smart? I'll take that plea deal you hinted at if you help me rescue Uncle John. He's been kidnapped! I hope you can find out who's behind this and where they might've taken him. To you he's only a zombie, but *we* love him dearly."

"I told him nobody in this police department listens to me! I wish they did, but --"

"He's a human *being*, damn it, and it's your *duty* to help us!"

"I think I know where he's been taken," Jane said after a thoughtful pause. "I had an undercover guy planted in a zombie hunting camp, but he must've been found out and killed. So I planted another one. I'll see if I can hook up with him and get the latest scoop."

"We need a ton of cops on this," Cy-Fi said adamantly. "Probably even police helicopters and a SWAT team!"

"I'll see what I can do," Jane said. "But I may have to go it alone."

She punched off and after thinking everything over, she buzzed the Chief of Detectives. When she told him what was happening, he didn't respond well. He said, "We were denied a warrant against Stush Polanski, surely you remember that, Jane. That sleaze-bag is too well-connected. Our hands are tied."

She wished she could tell the chief what she had learned from her latest informant, but he had not approved the tactic. She had done it on her own, knowing that if she made a request through the proper chain of command it would never have gotten approved. Therefore she was stuck. She couldn't admit to the chief that she had gone behind his back.

Desperately, she said, "But this is a *kidnapping*, Chief. A new wrinkle. We ought to be able to do *something*."

"Uncle John isn't alive," the chief said, "so technically it's not a kidnapping. It's a theft."

"But there are laws against theft of a corpse, Chief!"

"And I'd look damned ridiculous if I called out dozens of my men plus a SWAT team and helicopters to go out hunting for a missing corpse, especially a zombie. Forget it, Jane. You're asking me to go out on a limb."

Jane wanted to tell him to grow a pair of balls, but she refrained.

She put on a bulletproof vest and checked her Beretta automatic to make sure the clip was full and a round was already in the chamber. Then she practically ran out the door and jumped into her car.

CHAPTER 23

Caged in Stush's Lair

While Jane, Cy-Fi and Oscar were in a dither, I was still in the hunting lodge, locked in that little cage on casters, with barely room to do pushups. I was worried that if I went a long time without exercising, the rigor mortis would come back permanently. But at least I wasn't hungry. My little snack in the burlap sack had tided me over.

Stush gloated at me as he stood over his card table, piling loads of bundled-up cash into a satchel. It looked like he was intending to take the money and run. But what was going to happen to me in the meantime?

I was getting sick, not only from worry but from having to listen to hours and hours of Faux News. I refused to watch it by turning my head away, but I couldn't turn down the sound. The President was being investigated for possible collusion with a foreign country to undermine his opponent in the campaign that got him elected. I pretty much believed that he had done so because it was entirely in accordance with his character or lack thereof. Before he ran for the presidency he had started a fake university with his name on it, got hit with a class-action suit by the people he defrauded and had to settle it for twenty-five million dollars to keep from going to prison. His modus operandi for his real estate empire was to cheat all his suppliers and contractors out of the money he owed them, then declare bankruptcy. He had bankrupted parts of his so-called multi-billion-dollar enterprises at least six times. He was flagrantly enriching himself by means of his presidency but nobody knew how much because he was refusing to release his tax returns. However, you would learn none of this by watching Faux News. National surveys had shown that its rabid viewers considered themselves to be the most knowledgeable concerning politics and current events, but tests had shown them to be the *least* knowledgeable! That is partly why I started my blogs and podcasts. I wanted to do something to combat such blatant, pervasive ignorance. I had achieved status as a world-renowned zombie and I wanted to use it for the public good.

But my altruistic ambitions would come to naught if I perished in Stush's zombie hunting camp. I couldn't think of any way out of my predicament. Nothing that I could do on my own, that is. Locked in that cage, I felt that somebody needed to come and save me, and I was pinning my hopes on Cy-Fi.

One of the hunters had started to become rather chummy with me, though. He was a big guy with a totally bald head and a wild beard, and he always wore a big holstered gun on a thick black belt with lots of loops filled with bullets. His name was Zeke Corrigan. He'd come into the lodge from time to time, sit down and have a beer with Stush, then pull his chair over to the cage for a chat with me.

"You're a good conversationalist," he told me. "I'm not a dummy, I had two years of college -- phys-ed major, but I dropped out. Didn't flunk though, just had low grades. You're no dummy either, even though you're a zombie. I enjoy talking to you. I don't think you're gonna be around long, though."

I thought this last thing he said was entirely too cruel. It showed that in his heart of hearts he wasn't really much better than the other thugs. But I entertained a vague hope that if I could work on him a bit in the right way, dope him out and play him in reasonably clever ways, he might somehow be cajoled into helping me escape. Cy-Fi and I had accumulated a lot of money by now. So maybe he could be bought.

I didn't know that Jane Smart had already phoned Cy-Fi back at FLSH-TV, and told her where I was being held. I also didn't know that she had learned this and more from my erstwhile "pal" Zeke Corrigan.

"Oscar and I are on our way!" Cy-Fi blurted.

"No! Let me handle this!" Jane said.

"You already said the other cops won't help. You're gonna *need* us. We're heading out. We have a slew of weapons at our place, and we'll stop and get them."

"If you just go in blind, Stush and his guys will ambush you. You won't save Uncle John, you'll be his death warrant."

"Well, we're going! We can't just sit on our hands!"

That was my niece being her impetuous self. Whether she was doing the right thing or not, in retrospect I would have appreciated her wanting to try her best for me. But I would've expected no less from her.

While all that was going on without my knowledge, back at the lodge I got another big surprise -- Mandy Frost barged in, all smiles, and came over to Stush and kissed him on his cheek. I was aghast, as you can imagine. They were acting like bosom buddies, for God's sake! She even eyed the satchel full of money and fingered it with a proprietary air as if part of it belonged to her.

She sat at the card table and Stush chided her, but mildly. "You're late, Mandy. We're about ready to get the show on the road."

"Hey, I work at FLSH-TV, I can't just come and go as I please. Remember that without me you'd still be poor and rotting in a prison cell. By the way, where's Munch? He didn't show up at the station today."

With a sly smirk, Stush said, "I have a feeling the pressure was tearing him apart. He seems all torn up lately."

He winked at Mandy and she picked up on what he meant. So did I. I would have bet that Munch had been fed to the zombies outside in the big cage.

Mandy didn't appear to be very much moved by the realization. All she said to Stush was, "I have a feeling you're trying to tell me something."

"Yeah," he said. "Sometimes you can have one partner too many, know what I mean?"

"A two-way split is better than a three-way split," she agreed, smiling at him.

Stush said, "We're better off without Steve if he ain't gonna hold hisself together."

"Stop with the puns already, I get your point," Mandy squelched. "I already figured on something like this, so I hired another cameraman for today."

Stush said, "I want good coverage on everything that goes down. That way we'll sell a shitload full of DVD's."

Mandy got up and came over to the cage. She looked at me with something that almost passed for pity and said, "Poor Uncle John. You're not long for this world, but thank you for

boosting my ratings."

She had revealed herself to be an evil bitch, and I would never have suspected it. Maybe I *was* partly brain dead to have allowed her to pull the wool over my eyes all that time.

"I might as well tell you the truth," she said. "Nothing you can do about it anyway. We're going to make a fortune off of your putrefied hide. A pack of rich hunters have paid us big bucks for the thrill of hunting you down."

That's how I learned what my fate was intended to be. I felt just as scared as anyone else would be, even non-zombies. I was panicked that I'd never get to see my niece and nephew ever again and that all my plans for trying to do something to help save the country would just flat-out fade away and die.

I heard a bunch of vehicles screeching up outside with a lot of door banging and drunken yelling. Then about fifteen hunters barged into the lodge where Stush and his men had set up a keg of beer and a plank counter full of hard liquor with plastic glasses, ice and mixers. They kept on swilling booze, laughing, conning each other and getting drunker and drunker. They were all heavily armed with hunting rifles, side arms, knives and machetes. Some were in regular hunting garb and some were wearing camouflage. Some of them banged on the little cage I was in and hurled insults at me.

The hunters' drunken banter was all about guns and hunting and what a nice fall day it was for a hunt, and how much they enjoyed killing zombies. One elderly guy said his wife and kids were eaten up by zombies and that's why he liked to kill as many as he could from then on out. Well, at least I could empathize with that, even though I didn't like the fact that he was going to take it out on me.

A young dude with a mean scowl on his face said, "I don't have any particular grudge to hold onto, I just shoot 'em 'cause it's so much fun! Hell of a lot more challenging than just puttin' holes in targets! At least they move around and you have to follow 'em with your sights, then squeeze your trigger slow and easy-like."

"Seduce it, don't rape it!" someone called out. "That's what they told us over and over on the firing range in the army!"

"Yeah, Buddy!" another guy sounded off. "If you jerked your trigger-finger too much and couldn't get a high enough marksman rating, they made you tape Kotex to the butt and called you a pussy!"

Two of the drunkest hunters started messing with the cage and realized that the cage would roll and they started shoving it around and around, making me dizzy and got a big kick banging me from side to side against the bars. "Hey! Cut it out!" I yelled, but nobody paid any attention.

I noticed Zeke Corrigan looking on at this and stroking his beard thoughtfully. I didn't know what he was thinking but I hoped it was somehow to my benefit. Maybe he felt sorry for me and would do something to help.

A big burly hunter wearing amber shooter's glasses called out, "Hey, Stush, let's get this thing started! I hope it's worth the big bucks we're shellin' out!"

Stush said, "All right, enough levity -- let's get Uncle John outta the cage." He unlocked it and barked, "C'mon outta there, you brain-dead fuck!"

Joe and Judy, all decked out for the hunt, came at me with cattle prods and I said, "No, don't! I'll do what you say."

But they both zapped me anyway, on my belly and legs. And they didn't stop even after I complied. They prodded me out the side door of the lodge and toward the big cage. Its gate was hanging open, and the zombies that had been in there, ten or twelve of them, were being herded out, all except three or four they were probably going to keep so more people could be turned into zombies by being captured and bitten.

A couple of hunters kept yelling, "Shoo! *Shoo!*" and poking at the zombies with long bamboo poles.

Stush said, "Git along, little dogies! *Haw!*"

The rest of the hunters poured out of the lodge to laugh and jeer at the zombies, including me. One of the most boisterous, a guy named Jocko, drew his pistol. "Stand back and gimme room!" he said. "I'll get these tenderfeet dancin'!"

He started firing bullets at the zombies' feet, not to hit them but to keep them moving across flat ground and up a hill. They headed in the direction he wanted them to, in order to get away from loud gun blasts and bullets puffing into the earth.

Judy called out, "Way to go, Jocko!"

Joe said, "It don't make no never mind if we wing one in the foot or even in the knee -- none of 'em can feel pain!"

Laughing, Judy said, "Jocko likes to play cowboy!"

Some of the other hunters started firing over the zombies' heads, but Jocko kept aiming pretty close to their feet.

"Stop that shit!" Stush yelled. "You guys paid to go after *active* targets, not crippled ones!"

"Damned straight!" one of the hunters agreed. "Don't spoil 'em for givin' us a good chase!"

A few sporadic shots rang out, then the firing stopped.

"Now get Uncle John movin' up the hill!" Stush said.

Joe and Judy started zapping me again with their cattle prods. Those damned things hurt! *Zap! Zap! Zap!* I thought they were going to set my clothes on fire. I hurried the best I could to catch up with the other zombies. How was I ever going to survive? These hunters probably thought they were vastly superior to me in every way, but I still had a conscience and they didn't, and they fully intended to hunt me down and shoot me like a mangy dog.

While they were all down near the big cage waiting for Stush to tell them the hunt was on, Oscar and Cy-Fi pulled into the woods behind the lodge. They got out of the Le Mans and heard the gunfire a distance away.

"Omigosh, we're too late!" Cy-Fi said. "They're shooting zombies already!"

She opened the car trunk and grabbed a lever-action Winchester rifle from a pile of weapons.

Oscar said, "I need somethin' better'n my teeny-weeny pistol, Sis." She handed him an AK-47.

Just then Jane Smart pulled up in a squad car. Cy-Fi brightened with relief as Jane got out of the vehicle. "Detective Smart!" she said. "I'm so glad you're here! They're going to martyr Uncle John if we don't stop them! Where are the SWAT guys and the helicopters?"

"They're not coming," Jane said, shaking her head sadly.

"*What?!* Please don't tell me that! What's their excuse?"

"None of them believed me. They said I was going off half-cocked. I think it's because I'm a woman, damn their eyes!"

Oscar mumbled, "If you're a woman how can you go off half-cocked?"

Jane and Cy-Fi ignored him.

Jane said, "My boss doesn't think zombies are any kind of threat anymore. He doesn't think Uncle John is for real. And he doesn't think he can get a warrant against Stush Polanski -- the guy who's running this godforsaken place."

Cy-Fi said, "I googled it on the way here. Folks have been disappearing from this neck of the woods for *months* now! What does your boss say to that?'

"He says it's because nobody wants to stay on their farms anymore. The natural gas wells have made some of them rich as hell and the rest are too poor from working worn-out soil."

"The gunshots from down there have died down," Cy-Fi said. "If they haven't already killed Uncle John, we have to rescue him, no matter what happens."

Down by the cage, after Stush had given the order to temporarily suspend firing, Mandy

Frost showed up with a young guy toting a big TV camera and a heavy tripod. "This is Mike, my new cameraman," she told Stush. "He's gonna replace Munch."

"What're you waitin' for, Mandy? You two should be documentin' this whole thing!"

"Okay already!" Mandy snapped back. "C'mon, Mike! Leave the tripod. We'll hand-hold everything from up on the hill."

Mike leaned his tripod against a tree, then caught up with Mandy, and they hustled after the zombies. "I see Uncle John!" Mandy said. "He's trying to hide behind a bush!"

Watching Mandy and Mike start their climb, Stush said to Judy, "Let's get ready for the wrap-up. I don't think it's gonna take too long -- these men are sharpshooters. When they come back in they'll be braggin' and yellin', fulla spit and vinegar and mighty hungry. So you and Joe go fire up the grill and start cookin' the burgers and dogs. Did you make the potato salad, like I asked you?"

"I made a huge bowl full."

"Good, babe."

He saw that the hunters were all getting antsy, anxious to make kills. But he didn't want the hunt to be on till the zombies had a chance to get all the way up the hill and into the woods. Some of the hunters liked the danger of having to flush them out, even though sometimes the zombies got the upper hand.

Stush told Joe and Judy, "I'm gonna leave you two in charge while I check things out up at the lodge. Wait at least ten more minutes before you let these guys start goin' up there after the zombies."

"Right, boss," Joe said.

"Don't start getting into my potato salad before anyone else," Judy joked.

Stush faked a laugh. He had his mind on what he was going to secretly do, which was to take the satchel full of money and split while everybody else was preoccupied.

Meanwhile, Jane, Oscar and Cy-Fi had worked themselves into a position where they could take cover behind a shed and peep out to observe the goings-on down by the cage and past it, up the hill.

Oscar said, "What're we gonna do, Sis? Looks like we're outnumbered."

Thinking quickly, Jane came up with a plan. "We should try to arrest them right now while we have our best chance. once the hunt is in full swing and they're all scattered around in the woods, we'll have a devil of a time rounding them up."

Oscar said, "What about the zombies? How're we gonna round *them* up, Sis?"

Cy-Fi said, "If we can rescue Uncle John, he'll help us out. We can use him to lead the others to safety. He'll become the Pied Piper of Zombies, so to speak."

"Let's get a move on," Jane said. "Before those guys down there start picking their way up the hill and into those woods."

They skirted the woods around to the back of the cage, then Jane stepped out into plain view, flourishing her badge and pointing her pistol. "Halt right there, fellows!" she called out. "This hunt is over!"

Some of the hunters froze, but others faced Jane, shouldering their rifles or pulling out their side arms.

From halfway up the hill, Mandy Frost saw and heard what was happening. Angry at the unforeseen intrusion into her money-making scheme, she started yelling. "I don't know who this broad is, but *shoot her! She's trespassing!*" Mandy had plenty of trepidation about killing a cop, but she was cornered and desperate enough to put that aside.

Oscar and Cy-Fi still had not shown themselves. They were hiding behind some big boulders near the cage but out of sight of the hunters. "We have you surrounded!" Jane lied. "We're the law! There are a lot more of us behind me! A SWAT team is on the way! Throw down your weapons!"

Reluctantly, they all started to comply -- but slowly -- except for Jocko.

"She's bluffing!" Mandy cried out. "I don't see anybody but her from up here! *Shoot* her!"

Jocko wasn't sure what to do. He hesitated, then started to swing his rifle barrel toward Jane.

A loud shot rang out.

Jocko clutched his chest and fell dead.

Cy-Fi worked the lever action of her rifle as she ducked back down behind a boulder. Her barrel still smoking, she yelled, "You're disgusting, Mandy! You better make a run for it because I'm going to *kill you!*"

Mandy didn't give up trying to make the hunters obey her. She shouted at them, "You hear her? She's *crazy!* Grab up your guns and *open fire!*"

Cy-Fi threatened, "You better not!"

Jane took advantage of the slight lull and ran back behind the boulder where Cy-Fi was.

The hunters dove for their weapons and Oscar, Cy-Fi and Jane opened fire. They had the advantage of cover, and quickly scored some kills. Five hunters went down and the other six took off running, taking cover behind trees, rocks and boulders. A tremendous fusillade erupted.

Up at the lodge, Stush was alarmed. Surely the zombie hunt didn't start yet? And why would all that firing be taking place at once? He came out the side door and looked, then muttered to himself, "Holy shit! We're under attack!" He saw three hunters running, trying to make it up the hill and into the woods, but one of them was hit and went down hard. The other two looked like they were going to get away. Then Stush saw Mandy and Mike the cameraman hustling back down the hill. They both seemed to be making it to safety -- but a large, vicious male zombie in bibbed coveralls stepped out from some tall weeds and grabbed at Mike, making him drop his camera. The zombie wrestled Mike to the ground and took a huge, stringy, bloody bite out of his cheek.

Mike screamed his head off, and so did Mandy, he out of the pain of being bitten, she out of shock and fear. She abandoned him and ran for her life.

Two more zombies joined in the feast, tearing Mike apart.

Stush had seen more than enough. His instinct, as always, was to save himself and to hell with others. He had already intended to get the hell out of there with all the money, but now he moved as fast as he could. He grabbed the satchel from his secret cubbyhole and drew his revolver in case he had to battle his way out.

Joe and Judy barged in on him.

"Where do you think you're going, Stush?" she demanded angrily.

He pointed his revolver at her, saying, "I got all the money. I'm gettin' the hell outta here."

"Hey, what about *us?*" Joe said.

"Screw you, I'm travelin' light!" Stush said.

He plugged both Judy and Joe with two pistol shots in rapid succession and they both fell, clutching their wounds. Judy fell halfway under the card table. Joe was hit in his throat and fell backwards against a log wall, blood streaming between his fingers as he went down.

Stush said, "Fuck you both, gonna leave you for zombie feed!"

He dashed outside, jumped into Joe's van and tossed the satchel full of money on the passenger seat. Obviously he intended to jump in and peel out -- but he never got to do it. Judy staggered out of the lodge, bleeding from a chest wound, and shot him in his head. Then she fell down and died. She wasn't ghoul bitten and neither was Joe, so they'd end up as zombie feed before long if the ghouls found them while they were still fresh.

Shots were still ringing out as the battle raged on down near the big cage. Jane, Oscar and Cy-Fi had to see it through before they could try to find me and make me safe. At the same time, I was trying my best to save *myself.* I scrambled onto a path down the hill, a roundabout path some distance from the vicinity of the cage -- and I spotted Mandy Frost running down the hill on that same path but pretty far ahead of me. I decided to just follow behind her if I could. But I was a lot slower than she was. A couple of zombies came at her from behind a brick wall, and she shrieked but was able to narrowly dodge them because they were the usual slow-moving kind, probably with rigor mortis, like me. I got past them with no trouble because they wouldn't want to eat their own kind, which was pretty decent of them, wouldn't you say?

When Mandy got to the bottom of the hill, I saw her head for the lodge and so, just by some sort of instinct, I kept following her. She had done her best to do me dirt, and I harbored an intuition that my fate would be tied to hers till the bitter end.

She came upon Joe's van, the same one that had been used to kidnap me. Stush lay beside it, looking dead. I didn't totally realize his condition right away, though, because at first I wasn't close enough. I watched Mandy stop in her tracks and take a long time eyeing Stush's body. Then she saw the satchel lying half under him. She tugged on it to get it free of his weight, then popped it open and saw that it was packed full of bundled-up currency. She smiled gloatingly and said, "Thank you, Stush!"

Totally pleased with herself, she darted quickly toward a little red Mazda that must've been hers, but I blocked her path. She gasped when she saw me, then backed away, pleading with me. "Please, Uncle John, you don't want to hurt me, do you? Please, honey...I never meant to harm you...I made you famous. Please don't hurt me, Uncle John..."

"I won't bite you," I said. "Your flesh would be bitter to me. But I can't say the same for my friends."

So saying, I jumped at her and she wheeled to run -- and bounced off the chest of a big, grizzled zombie who had been coming at her from behind. He stared into her eyes as his hands clamped tightly around her throat. She dropped the satchel full of money. I looked on as the big zombie choked her and dragged her down. Then more zombies closed in, single-mindedly hungry for her. They knelt over her and started biting and chewing, tearing her apart. I knew that they had to eat and that what they were doing, in a certain sense, was no more appalling than lions and tigers having to bring down and feast upon a young, tasty impala.

I was rooted in my tracks for a moment, uncertain as to where to hide or what to do next. Gunfire was still coming from where the big cage was, so I was scared to go down there. It would be a useless move. There was nothing I could do at the moment to help Jane Smart or my niece and nephew.

Then a gruff voice said, "Don't make a wrong move, Uncle John!" Startled, I thought I knew the voice. I slowly turned around and saw that I was right. It was Zeke Corrigan, who I thought had some empathy for me when I was caged. He had a pistol in one hand and a cattle prod in the other. "We're goin' on a little trip in Joe's van," he said with a chortle. He opened the cargo door and there was a really big dog cage in there, and he forced me to get in by zapping me over and over with the cattle prod till I hurried up and did as I was told. Then he locked the door of the dog cage on me and I was cramped inside of it like a poorly treated zoo animal. I didn't know what more he was going to do to me, but I hoped that Ci-Fi, Oscar or Jane would be able to stop him before my plight got much worse. My brain was so addled by now that I wouldn't have put it past him to put me on display somewhere and sell tickets.

He slammed the cargo door shut, jumped in behind the wheel and peeled out. I had no idea where he was taking me but I didn't think it would be to a picnic or a baseball game.

CHAPTER 24

After the Rampage

When all the shooting died down and the bad guys were all killed or captured, Jane and Cy-Fi, let alone Oscar, didn't quite know how to handle the aftermath. The last time they had seen me, I was being herded up the hill toward the woods. And presumably there were still quite a few other zombies on the loose up there.

Quickly thinking it over, Jane said, "We're going to need help. We can't let those creatures wander out of the woods and attack innocent people in their homes."

"But I don't like to see them shot down!" Cy-Fi said. "And I have to save Uncle John!"

"I'm with you, Sis!" Oscar said immediately.

"For my part, I'll agree to let your uncle alone," Jane said. "But dealing with the others is a big problem. Not just my boss but all the other cops will want to gun them down. They're not going to agree to just rounding them up. What on earth would they do with them? I know that you've been campaigning for hospitals and hospices, but nothing like that is in place yet, and it won't be, at least for the foreseeable future."

"We have friends, Sis," Oscar said plaintively.

Cy-Fi's eyes lit up. It was one of those out-of-the-mouth-of -babes moments. "Of course!" she said. "Our Zombie Protection Society!"

"What can *they* do?" said Jane.

"We don't *need* to call in the cops!" Cy-Fi enthused. "Sometimes you amaze me, Oscar! I can get lots of good honest people to come out here -- folks who're already kind enough to treat zombies like human beings."

"You mean...?" Jane said, shaking her head.

"Yes! That's exactly what I mean! Quite a few of our members are already hiding their infected relatives and taking good care of them. And some of the others probably wouldn't mind doing the same thing. It'd be like providing sanctuary for immigrants. I'm sure we can get it done."

"How many do you think we're dealing with?" Jane asked.

"When Oscar and I first got here we saw no more than seven or eight being herded up the hill, and Uncle John was one of them. He's got to be culled out of the group because he's more advanced than they are. Will you agree to that, Jane?"

Mulling it over, she said, "I suppose that's the right thing to do, all things considered, I just hope my ass doesn't get fired. I'll let him go home with you, if we can find him. I owe you that much. But he's got to remain constantly under your care. And I'll simply have to trust you to feed him...er...in the same selective way that you've been doing all along. If you can agree to that, then it's a deal."

"You've come a long way, babe!" Cy-Fi said elatedly.

She and Jane bumped fists.

Too bad I wasn't where they thought I was. Instead I was bouncing around in a dog cage in a van being driven by Zeke Corrigan toward some kind of unknown destination.

Meanwhile, over the next couple of hours Cy-Fi actually did get a dozen or so members of the Zombie Protection Society to come to the hunting camp and help round up the zombies in the woods. They weren't allowed to carry any firearms, just lassos, stun guns, handcuffs and shackles, and big human-sized nets like the kind used to capture gorillas. She headed up the search party to make sure nobody did me any harm. She wanted to be the first to embrace me once I was found.

While that was going on, Jane Smart and Oscar combed the grounds of the lodge and its immediate environs. They found the bodies of Judy, Joe and Stush. They also found the torn-up remains of Mandy Frost but didn't know at the time that it was she.

What they didn't find, either in the woods or at the lodge, was me.

However, once again Oscar supplied an avenue to pursue when he said, "That dead guy over there is one of the ones who kidnapped Uncle John. I didn't see his van out there, though."

"What kind of van was it?" Jane immediately asked.

"A black one with no signs on it, like any kind of business like a delivery van for a store or something. And I couldn't get the license plate. Like I told Cy-Fi, it was covered with mud."

"But you're pretty sure this guy was the owner of it?" Jane pressed.

"Pretty sure, yeah," Oscar replied.

"Anything else you can tell me about him?"

"Nuh-uh. I'm sorry, Jane."

"I've got to get to a computer," Jane said.

She knew she also had to come up with a cover story for what had gone on here. So,

after all the zombies loose in the woods up on the hill were captured and "adopted" by willing people, she used her cell phone to put in a call to the police station, and got the chief got on the phone. She reported that she had been brought to the camp by an anonymous tip and had arrived to find unfathomable carnage. Dead bodies all around, and lots of weapons.

"It looks for all the world like some kind of a terrible shoot-out took place here," she told the chief. "We're going to need a team of CSI investigators. Maybe even *two* teams."

She laid it on thick because she knew that he had a one-track mind and if she could get it focused where she wanted it to be, she'd have a better chance that he wouldn't delve any deeper.

"I'm telling you, Chief, this is a mysterious situation and it's going to need someone like you to figure it out."

"I don't need this kind of goddamn headache," the chief moaned.

Jane said, "It's not my fault, Sir. But I need you here, I really do."

He didn't reply to that. He just slammed the phone down.

Jane turned to Cy-Fi and said, "You and Oscar have to clear out. You heard me. The way I played it was that I came here all alone, on a tip. So you're home free so long as the chief never tumbles to you. I'd get rid of the weapons you fired, though, in case they take slugs out of the bodies lying around here that can give them a match."

"Good advice," Cy-Fi said, and she and Oscar got into the Le Mans and headed out of there in a big hurry.

CHAPTER 25

The Hope for a Good Outcome

After the shoot-out at Stush's hunting camp, Jane Smart underwent an intensive debriefing by the chief and two police force investigators she had worked with in the past. She didn't get home till after midnight and was unable to sleep. She tossed and turned, trying to rationalize her own feelings about all that had gone down. She felt guilty about her part in concealing some of the most important facts from her own colleagues.

The thing that made her feel better about what she had done was contemplating the loving and mutually protective relationship that Uncle John enjoyed with his niece and nephew. They were the epitome of "Family Values," a catch-phrase that was a cornerstone of the right wing in America, a knee-jerk precept that had often seemed to her to be honored more in the breech than in the observance. It had been violated again and again by hypocritically sinful televangelists who, after being found out in their homosexual or heterosexual dalliances, went before their congregations shedding crocodile tears and begging God to forgive them their sins.

Who knew whether or not God actually did it? He never came down from the clouds and made a public ruling. But the congregants themselves were amazingly forgiving of even the most vile and disgusting transgressions.

Jane decided that she ought to respect Cy-Fi and Oscar for what they were doing. She thought of her love for her own mother. What if her mom would have survived as a zombie? Would she have summoned the courage to dispatch her? Or would she have hidden her away and hoped for a cure someday, as Cy-Fi and Oscar had done for their beloved uncle?

As for Uncle John, who could say that he didn't have any value as a person? He was bright, introspective, undeniably knowledgeable and even ethical in his own way. He couldn't help what he had become. She was confounded that she had so much in common with a *zombie*. She meant his intellectual leanings, his political sentiments. He had a social conscience in tune with hers. If it weren't for his half-rotted face, she might even be romantically attracted to him. Looks aside, she had had worse dates. Many of the handsomest ones had also been the most insufferable, self-absorbed to the point of repugnance. At least Uncle John was intellectually stimulating even though he was also infuriating. (She was thinking this way about *me*, mind you, but at the time I had no way of knowing, because I was in a dog cage, miles away.)

The upshot of her soul-searching was that she felt a driving need to track me down and find out who had absconded with me. She knew that I must be in dire peril if not already done for. Having gone into battle with Cy-Fi and Oscar, she now didn't want them to have to grieve for me. She had come to feel, quite correctly in my estimation, that at heart my niece and nephew were good, decent people who had been forced by a unique circumstance into unusual but perhaps justifiable behavior.

So far, she had not revealed to anyone that she had had a snitch inside Stush's criminal enterprise: Zeke Corrigan. No trace of him had been found. So where was he? As of now, he was missing, and so was Joe Talerico's van. That could not be a coincidence, Jane thought. She had not told anyone that tons of money must be missing, too; the cash paid to Stush by his fat-cat hunters. She figured if she could recover that windfall she would contribute the bulk of it to the Zombie Protection Society and use the rest to finance an early retirement from the police force. She was sick of her job anyhow.

Morgue photos of the late Joe Talerico had been published in newspapers and on TV, and once his likeness had been identified by his younger brother, a local postal clerk without any criminal record, the registration and license plate number of Joe's missing van had been easily traced by Jane through the Pennsylvania Department of Transportation. Logic told her that Zeke must've made his escape in that same van and Uncle John must have been his hostage.

Her gut instinct was confirmed when Harvey Slocum, the getaway driver the day Betty Montgomery was kidnapped, got arrested while trying to rob a convenience store. He confessed to being a regular at Stush's zombie hunting camp and bragged about slinking into the woods during the shootout. During his initial interrogation, he was full of venom when Zeke Corrigan's name came up: "That motherfucker split in Joe's van and he wouldn't even let me get in, he just laughed and peeled out! We ever share a cell, I'll wring his fuckin' neck!"

A week or so before the shoot-out had gone down, Jane had made plans to join Cy-Fi, Oscar and Uncle John in a major political event scheduled for this coming weekend: a Million Person March on the nation's Capitol, in protest against the President's recent Executive Order giving law officers the right to arrest zombies and zombie impersonators on sight and force them to undergo medical testing, then have them "put to sleep" if they turned out to be for real biologically. So far, the Supreme Court had blocked enforcement by a five to four vote, but White House lawyers had gone to court to try to get the ruling overturned. The Million Person March in Washington, DC, with adjunct marches in many other cities, was a gigantic protest against this new infringement of civil liberty. It bore an eerie resemblance to the "stop and frisk" harassment of black people by cops in New York City. Also, the attempt several years ago to force women to take gynecological exams under the pretense that they needed to prove they had healthy genitals in order to be prescribed birth control pills. Of course the real reason was to stop as many women as possible from preventing pregnancy, and once pregnant to take away their right to an abortion.

Jane knew that Oscar and Cy-Fi were hoping that somehow Uncle John might be found and rescued, not only for his own sake, but for the joy it would bring him and his fans if he could be brought home safe and sound, but also so they all could take part in the Million Person March for zombie rights. His presence would be utterly inspirational.

Impelled by this strong motivation, Jane tried to think what she might do in the face of frustrating ambiguity about her next possible moves. There was already a BOLO out on Joe Talerico's van, a police Be On the Lookout bulletin. The chief had agreed to do this with little urging from Jane because he thought that whoever had taken the van might be guilty of worse crimes at the hunting camp. "But good luck finding it," he had ranted. "For God's sake, it could be anywhere!" He still didn't consider kidnapping Uncle John to be a serious crime, even though Uncle John was famous and highly missed by his legion of dedicated fans. "I'm not going to bust my ass trying to track down a so-called zombie!" he fumed to the media. "I've got a sight more important things to do with my undermanned police force!"

So Jane had to somehow carry on a totally unauthorized investigation behind the chief's back. The only avenue of pursuit that she could come up with was to try to pump information out of Zeke Corrigan's friends and relatives. They were an unsavory lot, ranging from lazy but relatively harmless louts to out and out gangsters. But she gritted her teeth and set her sights on questioning them one by one, whenever and wherever she might be able to find them.

At the same time, she had more hope for Cy-Fi's methods than for her own. Cy-Fi had mustered the full resources of the Internet, relentlessly working Uncle John's web site, blogs and Face Book pages. She paid for full-page newspaper ads and a sixty-second spot with a massive time-buy on FLSH-TV. She used Twitter and LinkedIn. And of course she implored the total membership of the Zombie Protection Society to join in the hunt for their hero, Uncle John.

All this was going on without my knowledge while I bounced over the ruts of a dirt road in a bone-jarring, ear-jangling dog cage. The cab door of the van opened, then slammed shut. Then Zeke pulled open the cargo door and looked in at me with a derisive grin that became a chortle. "Maybe I oughta leave you in here," he said. "Cage and all."

"Please don't," I said simply, figuring his sadistic streak might be tweaked if I whined about it. Best if I kept my voice devoid of emotion in his presence.

"Kids come around here with their be-be guns, they might hear you if you start groaning or kicking the cage." So saying, he lifted me out of there, cage and all, and carried me up three rickety steps onto the porch of an old shack with a tarpaper roof. He was incredibly strong, but he grunted when he set me down. Then he unlocked the weather-stripped door and dragged the cage inside with me still in it. He left me in the middle of the plank floor, went back out, and came back with his rifle and the satchel full of money.

"Startin' to drizzle out there," he remarked. "Gonna be one hell of a storm, accordin' to the weather report."

The shack only had one room. I didn't see any place set aside for a toilet, no cubbyhole or anteroom in sight, but in a corner there was an old porcelain kitchen sink, a hot plate on a card table and one folding chair. Zeke propped his rifle against the table, put the satchel on top of it,

sat down in the cushion-less chair, opened the satchel and started gleefully counting the money, un-banding it a stack at a time and making sure that the amounts tallied with what was written on the paper bands.

He didn't seem to care that I was as cramped as a sardine in that wire cage and aching all over with rigor mortis.

"Hah! Almost half a million bucks!" he shouted after an incredibly long time spent counting.

Lucky for me, he was greedy. Otherwise he would have been happy with the amount of cash he already had and would surely have killed me right then and there with a shot to the head. He actually said as much, right to my face. "It might seem like I oughta be more than satisfied," he concluded. "But half a mil ain't nothin' these days. I could gamble it away in no time. So I'm gonna hold you for ransom.

You and your ditzy sister are rich now, and your fans might be mostly poor, but they could come up with a big pile if they had to. I guess I oughta be able to charge them at least ten million bucks to get you back. Then, after they pay up, I won't honor my side of the deal. Too risky. I'll just do away with you and burn your body."

"Can you at least let me out of the cage for a while?" I asked humbly. "Just to stretch my legs and take a leak somewhere? I'm not dumb enough to try to get away. I'd never be able to outrun you."

He smirked and said, "I'll think about it."

Just then there was a crash of thunder, a visible lightning flash in one grimy cobwebbed window, and rain started pounding on the tarpaper roof.

"I ain't takin' you outside in that," Zeke said. "You'll have to hold it till the storm's over."

"I have to do number one and number two both," I told him. And he said, "You might have to just shit your pants."

"That's cruel."

"Well, I don't believe you anyway. Zombies shouldn't have to poop or pee. You're just wantin' to trick me into lettin' you outta the cage so you can try some kinda crazy stunt."

He was partly right. But not about my bodily functions, of which he was woefully ignorant and disrespectful.

CHAPTER 26

Oscar Feeling Sad and Helpless

It stormed all over southwestern Pennsylvania that day, and Oscar used an umbrella to walk toward his latest assignment as a security guard. It was in a mall. Usually he went in early so he could loaf around the food court and get a Big Mac and a big milkshake. But he didn't feel much like eating these days, even though he often said that he was a big man who didn't do well if he let himself go hungry. He didn't have much appetite because he was overcome with sadness over what might have been my fate and what his part in it might have been. Poor fellow. He was suffering greatly, and if I had been there I would have told him that I knew he had a good heart and would never intentionally let harm come to me.

He ran the day of my kidnapping again and again through his grief-addled mind, wishing things had unfolded differently and turned out happier. He could see that if only he had waited to put the plastic flowers in the ground till after I had finished raking the leaves, I wouldn't have ruined the flowers with the rake. Then he would not have left me by myself at Grandpa's grave, while he went to get more flowers.

He had told me that Grandpa was up in heaven watching over me, and he truly believed that. He kept asking himself why the old man couldn't have been a much better guardian angel.

But he also knew that in life Grandpa had been pretty forgetful. His mind would often wander in the middle of a sentence.

Oscar sat by himself in a corner of the food court, drowning in misery. Everybody else was having fun eating and drinking, playing their fingers over the keys of their cell phones and laughing and joking with one another, showing off photos and text messages. In a few minutes, on an empty stomach, he'd have to start making his rounds from store to store with an eye out for vandals, shoplifters and other types of mischief-makers.

He and Cy-Fi had made TV spots and Internet announcements and pleas for help locating the missing van, presumed stolen. At least, thanks to Jane Smart, they had not only been able to give a full description of the vehicle, but had also put the license plate number on-screen over and over. When he had fired shots at those bad guys who captured me, he recalled that the plate had been covered with mud. It was something they must've done on purpose.

He made himself leave the food court and start going around, patrolling the stores that had signed up for security services from the firm that employed him. He was extremely listless and really didn't feel like doing his job today. But he remembered how I had taught him, from the time he was a little boy, how important it is to always maintain a sense of responsibility.

Suddenly he heard a ruckus -- a scream and some running footsteps -- and he spun around, trying to see where the disturbance was coming from. Three young boys were running from a middle-aged woman in a clerk's uniform, and the boys were trying to get away from her with items they had apparently shoplifted. Two of them dropped their stolen goods -- a set of earphones and some DVD's -- which enabled them to run faster. But the third boy tried to hang onto what he had snitched -- a toy of some kind in a colorful box -- and so he was slower than the other two, and besides he was more overweight.

Of course Oscar was overweight, too, and he hadn't eaten all day. But he forced himself to run as hard as he could, panting and sweating, and after a dogged chase down the main arcade of the mall he caught the boy by the scruff of his neck.

"Lemme go! *Lemme go!*" the boy yiped. But Oscar kept a strong grip on him. He couldn't have been older than thirteen.

Once the boy stopped struggling, Oscar slammed him down onto a bench. Then he used his cell phone to summon a mall detective, who took over from there. The rest of Oscar's day was pretty much uneventful. But he still didn't get anything to eat.

Cy-Fi was going to pick him up, and when he got outside of the main entrance he started looking for her 1967 Le Mans. It had stopped raining hard but was still drizzling, and there were puddles all over the sidewalks. All the shrubbery was dripping and some of the ground was muddy.

"*Fatso! Fatso!*" a boy yelled -- and pelted Oscar with a mud ball.

"*Over here, Fatso!*" came another yell -- followed by a fusillade of mud balls.

Then the two boys ran like mad -- and Oscar could not possibly have caught up with them through the drizzle and the slippery pavement. They made a quick escape, and he knew they must be the two who had gotten away from him inside the mall. He felt even worse now that they had fooled him again.

He was embarrassed at how badly they had soiled his uniform. There was even mud on his badge -- and that made him think once again of the mud on the van's license plate.

Every now and then Oscar experienced a flash of what, for him, was brilliance. And now was one of those serendipitous times.

The last time he had seen his and Cy-Fi's pleas for help on TV something had struck him funny, but he couldn't put a finger on it. But now, recalling the flashing of Joe Talerico's license plate number over and over on the screen, he was hit with a flash of deja vu. He wouldn't have used that term for it, though. But now he somehow had a notion that the next spot they put on the air ought to put more emphasis on the mud instead of the letters and numbers.

He told Cy-Fi his idea as soon as she pulled up in the Le Mans. But she was already excited about something else: upon getting into the car to go and pick Oscar up, she had found a ransom note inside a plastic bag tucked under one of the windshield wipers. The plastic bag was obviously to protect the note from the rain. She extracted it and read it once she got behind the wheel. It said: I HAVE UNCLE JOHN. I WANT TEN MILLION DOLLARS. YOU HAVE TEN DAYS TO RAISE IT. DON'T GO TO THE POLICE. THAT INCLUDES YOUR DYKE BED BUDDY JANE SMART. (I still have the note. At the time, Cy-Fi kept it for evidence and now that we don't need it anymore, I keep it as a souvenir. It annoyed me that he called Jane a dyke. I have nothing against anybody's sexual preference; live and let live. But I know for a fact that Jane is heterosexual.)

Concerning the note, Cy-Fi said, "Don't you see, Oscar? -- this means Uncle John must be someplace close by. Close enough for somebody, probably this Zeke Corrigan guy, to come here and plant the note -- unless he's in this with somebody else. I'm proud of you, bro! I think your idea is great, and I think we should put it to use with our Zombie Protection Society members, like we did when we had to round up the loose zombies at the hunting camp."

Oscar was still guilt-ridden and depressed, but a touch of pride kept into his demeanor.

Sheepishly he said, "You really mean it, Sis? You're proud of me? Even though I screwed up with the plastic flowers and all?"

She gave him a kiss on his chubby cheek and told him soothingly, "There's evil in the world, honey, and we can't always overcome it or protect ourselves from people's devious ways. But you're the best brother in the world and I would never trade you for anyone else."

CHAPTER 27

The Misery at the Cabin

Even though it was still pouring down rain, Zeke went out, banging the cabin door shut and locking it. Then he drove away in the van and was gone for about an hour. I didn't know where he went at that time, but later deduced that he must have been delivering the ransom note. He left me all cramped up in the dog cage, my joints aching and my arms and legs going numb, which wasn't entirely from insipid rigor mortis -- even a normal person would've gone numb. All the while my stomach was growling but I was in too much pain and jeopardy to allow myself to dwell on that, even though I hadn't had anything to eat since the nibbles in the burlap sack. The worst part was how badly I needed to relieve myself. I don't know how I managed not to soil my trousers while Zeke was gone; I even found myself hoping he'd come back soon, even though he was so hateful and disgusting. I knew about Stockholm Syndrome from my work as a historian, and I didn't want to descend to that level; instead I willed myself to stay alert for a chance to escape, though it seemed impossible.

Finally, when he came back, his mood had lightened. "Hot-diggety!" he said. "You think I ain't smart? Everything's goin' accordin' to plan!"

"I never said you aren't smart," I told him. "I used to kind of like you."

"I got a good heart, but I'm desperate," he admitted. "Gotta take advantage of my big chance, and you're it."

He stared at me in the cage for a long moment. Then he said, "I guess I can't stand you stinkin' up the cabin."

He got me out of the cage at gunpoint and tied a rope around my neck. Then he led me outside in the rain and gave me a chance to pee and poop. He even gave me some old yellowed wrinkled-up newspapers to use to wipe myself. We both got soaked. But the good thing was that I was able to wet some pieces of newspaper to get myself clean. He snorted when he saw the greenish tint of my waste products and started calling me "Mr. Green Poop" instead of "Mr. Brain Dead." With inner sarcasm, I told myself that I didn't know which of the two epithets I treasured more.

After I was done with my ablutions, such as they were, he herded me back into the cabin and tied me to the plumbing under the chipped porcelain sink. He trussed me up like a rodeo steer. Loops of rope were wrapped around my ankles and wrists, which were pulled up behind my back in such a way that if I struggled too much I'd strangle myself. He didn't care if that's what happened either. He had already taunted me that he wasn't planning on returning me to my niece and nephew still alive (or *half* alive, if you prefer to put that sort of label on my condition).

He gloated at me and said, "Don't worry, Mr. Green Poop, you ain't goin' *nowhere*."

Then he started drinking whisky and playing solitaire at the card table just a few feet away from me. Before long he fell into a drunken stupor. But this didn't give me any kind of opportunity that I could have seized on. I had already seen that there weren't any glasses on the sink or anywhere near it that I could've caused to fall and shatter, in hopes of getting a sliver that I could cut the rope with. If there had been, I would have taken chance on waking him up.

His rifle was propped in a corner, too far away for me to reach, and I was deathly sure that if I tried to wiggle across the floor to get to it, I'd likely strangle myself. And the rope was way too short anyhow; the part that had me leashed to the grimy U-shaped plumbing under the sink was only about three feet long.

Zeke was wearing a holstered pistol and a sheathed Bowie knife, but no way I could get to those either. Even if I could stretch far enough to touch them, he'd probably come to, and he wouldn't be too groggy to kill me.

I was so exhausted by all I had been through that I finally fell asleep on the floor, even though I was scared that if I writhed in the throes of a nightmare it might be another way that the rope could strangle me. I admit that before I succumbed to a fitful sleep I almost wanted to go

ahead and purposely struggle too much. I was that depressed.

When I came to, there were faint streaks of sunlight slanting through the dirty cobwebbed window high up. Dust motes were dancing in the rays. I realized that the rain must have ended and it was a clear sunny morning now.

Then I heard *PFFT! PFFT!* and *PING! PING!* -- coming from outside.

What on earth could be going on out there?

I remembered that Zeke had made mention of kids with bebe guns -- and it occurred to me that they must be taking potshots at his van. I must be hearing little brass pellets pinging off of the vehicle's metal bodywork and probably making little holes in the windshield and the rear and side windows. Boy, was Zeke going to be mad! And that wouldn't bode well for me.

When I heard boyish laughter and running feet, I figured those nasty kids must be making their getaway. Normally I hated vandalism, but this time I didn't give a damn except that it might enrage Zeke so much that he would just go ahead and shoot me in the head. On the other hand, he had lots of money now, and it wasn't his van but Joe's, who wasn't going to be driving it anymore. Zeke could buy any kind of new vehicle he desired, as soon as he finished ransoming me. So maybe he wouldn't be so angry after all.

***

Later that same day, Jane Smart was with Cy-Fi and Oscar at our house. They were having tea and cookies at the kitchen table. Jane had shown up worn out and discouraged. She explained that for five or six hours she had been pounding the pavement, hitting on all her snitches, doing her damnedest to track down and question Zeke Corrigan's relatives and pals.

"His dad's dead and his mom's an alcoholic," Jane said, stirring her tea. "The old crone looked so bad and smelled so *awful*, I swear she must not have had a bath since God knows when. She didn't even have her false teeth in, I saw them in a glass on the sink. She claimed she hadn't seen Zeke in over two years. She said he must not have needed a place to crash because that's the only time he ever showed up. Anytime he ever had some money in his pocket or anything good going on, he never came around. Then she worked herself into a bitter, drunken rant, she even admitted he was an accident and she didn't want a child in the first place but she got knocked up. She said it was a blessing to be rid of her husband and her son both. Thank God for small favors, was the way she put it."

"Did you have any luck anyplace else?" Cy-Fi asked.

"No, I dug up some of his cronies, and it was a tough gig. I basically had to flush them out, like hunting for roaches under a rock. None of them wanted to tell me anything. There's no honor among these mooks, but I got the feeling some of them believed Zeke might be about to make a big score. So they didn't want to rat him out, wanted to stay on his good side if they could. I put a lot of pressure on them but they didn't bend."

"Well," said Cy-Fi, "they could tell from the news reports and the TV spots we ran that Uncle John was kidnapped. It'd be a short leap, with you coming around to interrogate them, to put two and two together to add up to Zeke."

"Yeah, I could tell they were all secretly rooting for him, hoping there'd be something in it for them," Jane agreed.

Oscar piped up, saying, "Are you gonna tell her, Sis?"

"Tell me what?" said Jane with a grain of hope.

Cy-Fi said, "Big news. We got a ransom note." And she related how she found the note in a plastic bag tucked under the windshield of her 1967 Le Mans.

"That probably means Uncle John is being held close by," Jane said right away.

"That's what *we* figured," said Cy-Fi. "I'll tell you something else. Oscar came up with a good idea."

On hearing himself being praised, Oscar turned red and shyly looked away.

Cy-Fi told Jane about the new TV spot she had made that morning asking people to be on the lookout for the same van as before, same make, model and color, but with mud on the license plate so it couldn't be made out.

"We don't have just the TV spot running," Cy-Fi told Jane. "We've posted the same new information all over the Internet -- our blogs, podcast and Face Book pages, too. We made sure to hit the Zombie Protection Society as hard as we could."

"Well," said Jane, "let's hope it bears fruit. It may be our last best chance."

CHAPTER 28

Zombie Revenge

Darkness fell. My bladder was full. Zeke had given me nothing but a couple plastic cups of water all day long. I had to pee real bad, but he was making me hold it in. He wasn't making himself suffer, though. He had been drinking whisky and beer all day long and had gone outside umpteen times to relieve himself. Now he was almost drunk enough to pass out, but he had to pee one more time so he wouldn't piss his pants while he was in a stupor.

He went out onto the little rickety porch and pissed over the side, weaving and holding onto the banister as he did so.

It was a moonlit night and the cricket chirps were dense and loud. Nevertheless, he thought he heard an alarming sound. But what? He didn't go back inside for his rifle, but he drew his pistol from its holster.

"Who's out there?' he demanded, pointing his pistol all around.

In the glint of the moonlight he thought he saw splintery holes in the windshield of Joe's van. "Goddamn it!" he shouted. "I'll drill you kids if I catch you! You better come out and fess up to what you done!"

He got no response. Only silence, except for the cricket sounds.

He yelled again. "This ain't no *bebe gun*, I promise you *that!* Bebes *sting*, but this mother *kills!*"

He stepped down off the porch and prowled toward the van, confident that he would flush the kids out. And he'd smash their bebe guns against a tree, goddamn it, and break them in two!

I could hear all of Zeke's cuss words and threats from inside the house where I was tied up, under the sink.

"Holy fuck!" he said when he started to see the bebe holes up close.

He ducked down and saw shoes under the van, on the other side of it. It was a triumphant moment for him because now he figured that for sure he had the kids within reach. He would run them down if necessary and take their goddamn bebe guns. Hell, he'd even shoot them in the legs if he couldn't catch up with them. Then he'd finish the little shits off. After that he'd split the fuck outta here and hole up someplace else till he could collect his ransom money. Fuck it. He'd be so rich he could get away with damn near anything. Anybody ever came close to nailing him, he'd just pay them off. Money was power and he'd never get caught. Never go to prison again. That's for damn sure!

He pretended to turn away from the van for a few steps, just to fake the kids out so they'd stay put. Then he charged around the side of it with his pistol cocked and ready to fire.

But there were no kids with bebe guns -- instead there were four *zombies!* -- and in the shock of the moment he still managed to squeeze the trigger only to have the shot go wild.

The zombies clawed at him furiously, and the pistol dropped out of his hand. They pushed him to the ground and started biting into him everywhere he wasn't clothed. Then they began ripping his clothes away and ripping at his flesh.

Through all this he caught a glimpse of Jane Smart standing by, aghast, watching the zombies do their awful work.

"*Help me!* Please *help* me, Jane!" he cried out.

"Too late, you're already bitten," she stated with eerie calmness.

Out of the corner of his eye, as his visual ability started to fade, he thought he saw Oscar and Cy-Fi going up onto the porch of the cabin, but in his final seconds of thought he wondered if it were a hallucination. He felt other people standing by too, people who were not zombies. Then the pain of being chewed apart and ripped apart took over.

I couldn't contain my joy when Cy-Fi and Oscar rushed in to untie me. Oscar couldn't restrain himself from blurting out part of their side of the story as he and Cy-Fi undid the knots. Later I learned all the interesting and exciting details from them and from Jane.

The two kids with the bebe guns had seen the TV spot on that described the van and the possibly mud-besmirched license plate. What stood out most in their minds was the mention of a fat reward. They debated whether they could say anything to their parents without having their bebe guns taken away. But in the end they decided that they'd be forgiven because of the fifty-thousand dollars their parents could claim. Therefore they confessed what they knew and what they had done -- and the parents got in touch with the Zombie Protection Society.

Four of the families who had adopted zombies from Stush's hunting camp volunteered to bring their zombies with them to help rescue me. They were having trouble finding enough of the proper sort of food for their adoptees to eat, so the deal they offered was that in return for their help they would get not just the reward but also the "food."

I must confess that I ate a bit, too. I felt that I deserved it.

Poor Zeke. He didn't get his reward. But I got mine.

CHAPTER 29

All's Well that Ends Well

Mandy Frost was replaced at FLSH-TV by a colleague who got promoted into prime time by taking over *Frontline*, which used to be Mandy's show. This is a transcript of the show that introduced the new host, Jenny Blaze:

"Ladies and gentlemen, Uncle John seems to have gone back into seclusion after a shocking eruption of violence at the zombie hunting camp run by career criminal Stush Polanski, who was found partially devoured. Video evidence of the massacre was gleaned from a blood-spattered TV camera found near the dead body of a freelance cameraman whose identity is being withheld. Viewers are advised that much of what we are about to show you is not for the squeamish.

"Uncle John was adjusting well to his public life before it came to an abrupt close. He was doing many of the everyday things we all take for granted such as reading a good book, smoking cigars, even going to the seashore.

"But now he has vanished, along with his niece and nephew, who both may have been killed and devoured at the hunting camp. Cy-Fi's body has never been found, and neither has Oscar's. Authorities can't find them and are hampered because they don't even know their real last names. They have disappeared amid speculation that they may have committed suicide out of despair over losing their infamous uncle.

"Uncle John will be sorely missed by his many fans and admirers. In the short months he was with us, he was bravely putting himself in terrible danger. Stush and his henchmen wanted to capture him and gun him down. Perhaps he escaped from there, and perhaps he did not, and perhaps he was never there at all. But police are aware that his niece and nephew were trying to enlist Detective Jane Smart to help rescue Uncle John when disaster struck.

"Unfortunately, Detective Smart has also disappeared after thirteen mostly exemplary years as a police officer. Please continue to watch *Frontline* with your new host, Jenny Blaze, for more on this intriguing international story!"

As you already know, FLSH-TV got quite a few of the facts wrong, which is usual for television -- but I still don't think that the Tweeter-in-Chief should keep on calling it "fake news." He just wants to cast as much doubt as he can on the media, hoping they won't be believed if the worst finally comes out about him. When he does that it undermines the Fourth Estate and all the institutions we depend upon to safeguard the health of our democracy.

Jane Smart agrees with me. We live together now. She tolerates my discolored complexion. I think she loves me, and I don't think it's because of my money. She and I are looking forward to participating in the Million Person March, the first march of its kind in human history that will include both regular people and zombies!

ABOUT THE AUTHOR

With over twenty books published internationally and nineteen feature movies in worldwide distribution, John Russo has been called a "living legend." He began by co-authoring the screenplay for NIGHT OF THE LIVING DEAD, which has become recognized as a "horror classic." His books on the art and craft of movie making have become bibles of independent production.

John Russo wants people to know he's "just a nice guy who likes to scare people" – and he's done it with novels and films such as RETURN OF THE LIVING DEAD, MIDNIGHT, THE MAJORETTES, THE AWAKENING and HEARTSTOPPER. He has had a long, rewarding career, and he shows no signs of slowing down.

For more information on John Russo, his books, movies, or official merchandise, visit www.TheJohnRusso.com.

For information on MY UNCLE JOHN IS A ZOMBIE! – THE MOVIE, visit www.MyUncleJohnIsAZombie.com.

IMAGES FROM

THE MOVIE

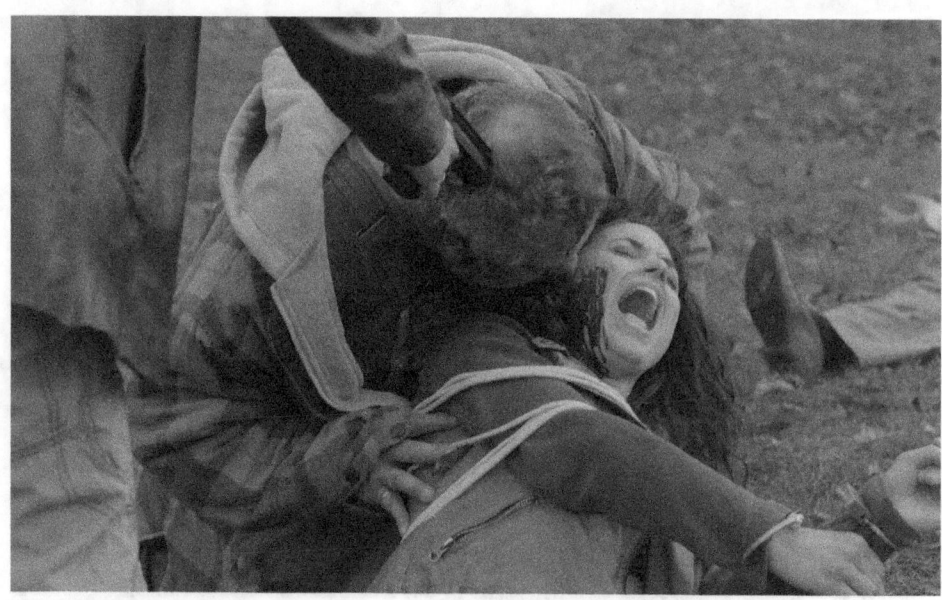

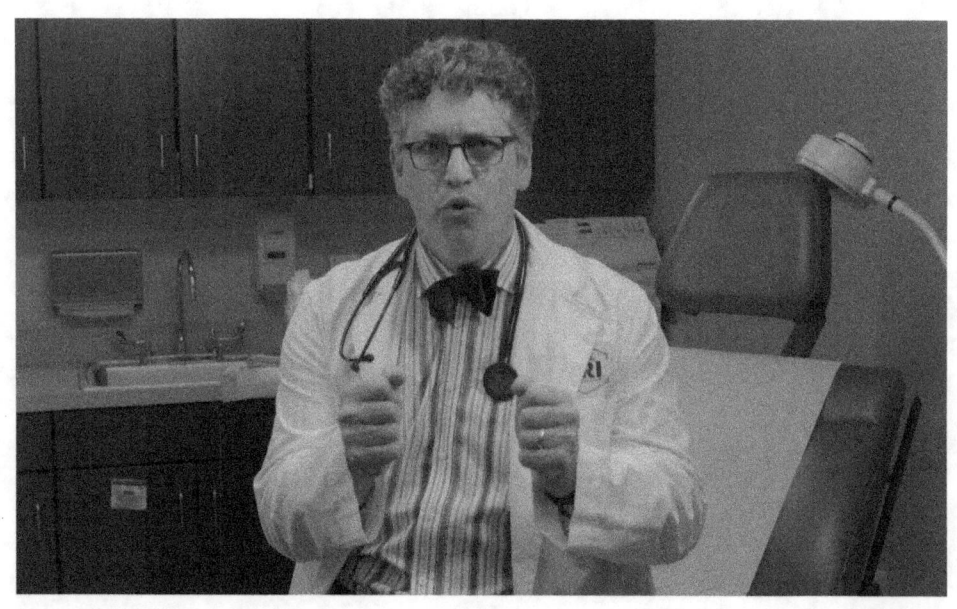

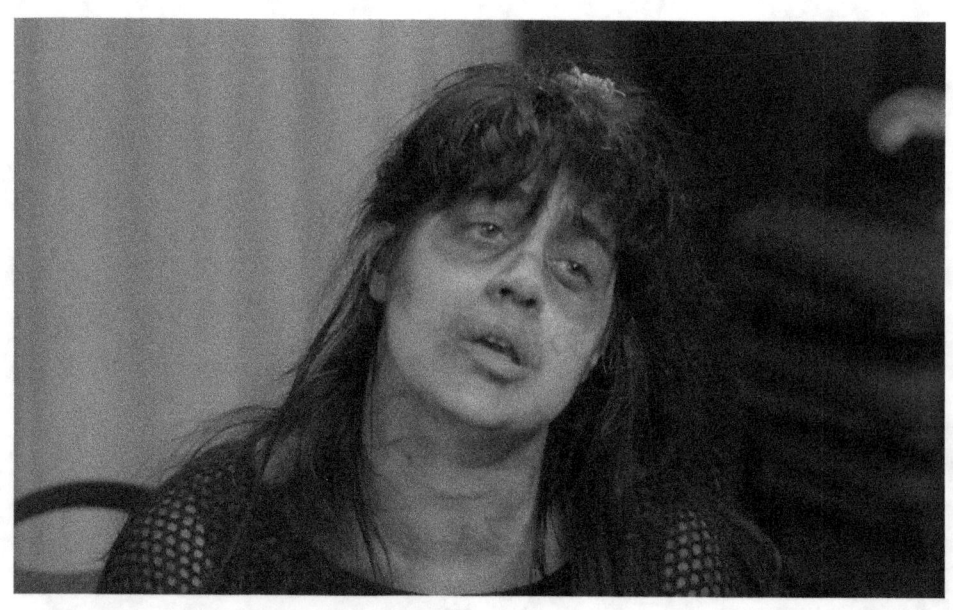

OTHER GREAT TITLES FROM

Burning Bulb

PUBLISHING

WWW.BURNINGBULBPUBLISHING.COM

night OF THE LIVING DEAD

JOHN A. RUSSO

RISE OF THE DEAD

AN EARTH-SHATTERING ANTHOLOGY OF ZOMBIE TERROR

Featuring Stories By:

John A. Russo   Tyson Blue   E.L. Stice   Nelson W. Pyles

Andy Rausch   Stephen Spignesi   R.D. Riley   Zakary McGaha

David J. Fairhead   Gary Lee Vincent   David C. Hayes   Rachel Montgomery

Paul Victor Wargelin   David F. Walker   William Vitka

Rich Bottles Jr.   Douglas Brode

ONE FAMILY'S LEGACY CARVED IN FLESH

BELLY TIMBER

A NOVEL BY

GARY LEE VINCENT SOLON TSANGARAS JOHN RUSSO

BASED ON A SCREENPLAY BY
KEN WALLACE & DUSTIN KAY

A WILD, WACKY, WONDERFUL, EPIC ZOMBIE NOVEL! - John Russo

DETOUR
TO ARMAGEDDON

SOLON TSANGARAS

Foreword by John Russo - Co-Creator of NIGHT OF THE LIVING DEAD™

THE FALL
OF TOMORROW

DAVID J. FAIRHEAD

DWELLING IN THE DARK

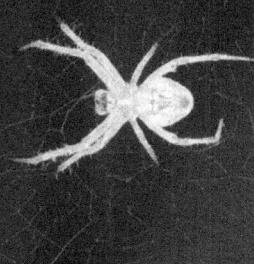

DAVID J. FAIRHEAD

The Hags of Black County

MICHELLE BOWSER

George Kosana
SAVE THE CROWS

GARY LEE VINCENT

PASSAGEWAY

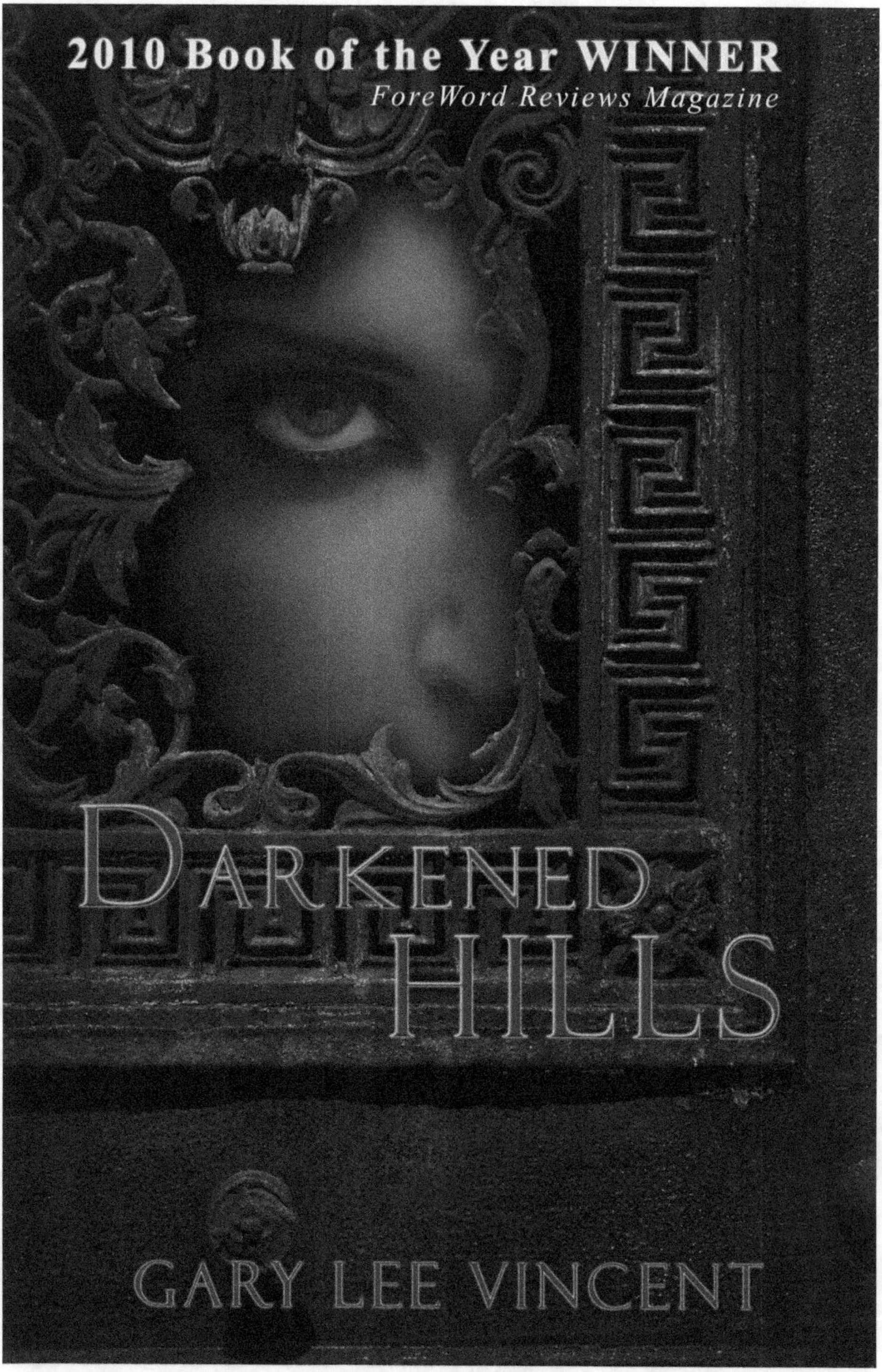
2010 Book of the Year WINNER
ForeWord Reviews Magazine
DARKENED HILLS
GARY LEE VINCENT

"I love a good vampire series and this one delivers in spades!"
- Brenda C. for Readers' Favorite

DARKENED HOLLOWS

GARY LEE VINCENT

Darkened Waters

Gary Lee Vincent

THE MOTHER OF DARKNESS HAS ARRIVED . . .

DARKENED SOULS

GARY LEE VINCENT

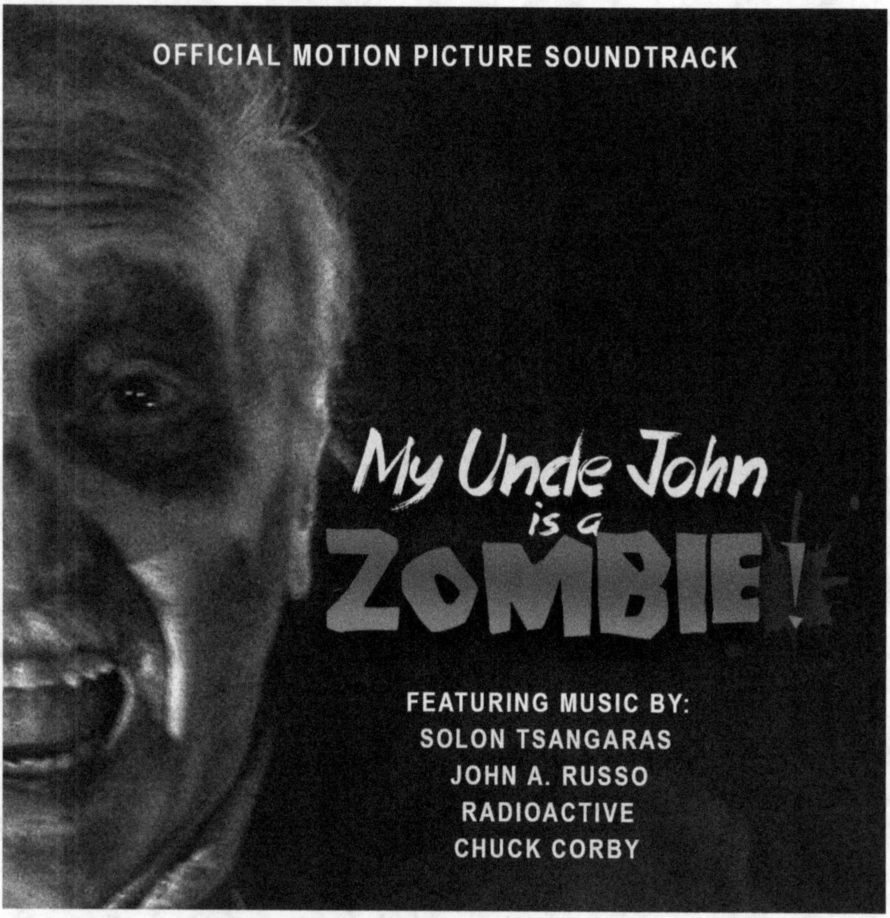